A Meet of Tribes

A Shade of Vampire, Book 45

Bella Forrest

Also by Bella Forrest:

THE GENDER GAME

The Gender Game (Book 1)

The Gender Secret (Book 2)

The Gender Lie (Book 3)

The Gender War (Book 4)

The Gender Fall (Book 5)

The Gender Plan (Book 6)

The Gender End (Book 7)

THE SECRET OF SPELLSHADOW MANOR

The Secret of Spellshadow
Manor (Book 1)

The Breaker (Book 2)

The Chain (Book 3)

The Keep (Book 4)

A SHADE OF VAMPIRE SERIES:

Series 1:
Derek & Sofia's story:

A Shade of Vampire (Book 1)

A Shade of Blood (Book 2)

A Castle of Sand (Book 3)

A Shadow of Light (Book 4)

A Blaze of Sun (Book 5)

A Gate of Night (Book 6)

A Break of Day (Book 7)

Series 2:
Rose & Caleb's story:

A Shade of Novak (Book 8)

A Bond of Blood (Book 9)

A Spell of Time (Book 10)

A Chase of Prey (Book 11)

A Shade of Doubt (Book 12)

A Turn of Tides (Book 13)

A Dawn of Strength (Book 14)

A Fall of Secrets (Book 15)

An End of Night (Book 16)

Series 3: The Shade continues with a new hero…

A Wind of Change (Book 17)

A Trail of Echoes (Book 18)

A Soldier of Shadows (Book 19)

A Hero of Realms (Book 20)

A Vial of Life (Book 21)

A Fork Of Paths (Book 22)

A Flight of Souls (Book 23)

A Bridge of Stars (Book 24)

Series 4:
A Clan of Novaks

A Clan of Novaks (Book 25)

A World of New (Book 26)

A Web of Lies (Book 27)

A Touch of Truth (Book 28)

An Hour of Need (Book 29)
A Game of Risk (Book 30)
A Twist of Fates (Book 31)
A Day of Glory (Book 32)

Series 5:
A Dawn of Guardians

A Dawn of Guardians (Book 33)
A Sword of Chance (Book 34)
A Race of Trials (Book 35)
A King of Shadow (Book 36)
An Empire of Stones (Book 37)
A Power of Old (Book 38)
A Rip of Realms (Book 39)
A Throne of Fire (Book 40)
A Tide of War (Book 41)

Series 6: A Gift of Three
A Gift of Three (Book 42)
A House of Mysteries (Book 43)
A Tangle of Hearts (Book 44)
A Meet of Tribes (Book 45)

A SHADE OF DRAGON TRILOGY :

A Shade of Dragon 1
A Shade of Dragon 2
A Shade of Dragon 3

A SHADE OF KIEV TRILOGY:

A Shade of Kiev 1
A Shade of Kiev 2
A Shade of Kiev 3

BEAUTIFUL MONSTER DUOLOGY:

Beautiful Monster 1
Beautiful Monster 2

DETECTIVE ERIN BOND
(Adult mystery/thriller)

Lights, Camera, Gone
Write, Edit, Kill

For an updated list of Bella's books, please visit her website:
www.bellaforrest.net

Join Bella's VIP email list and she'll personally send you an email
reminder as soon as her next book is out! Visit here to sign up:
www.forrestbooks.com

Contents

New Generation List

- **Aida:** daughter of Bastien and Victoria (half werewolf/half human)
- **Field:** biological son of River, adopted son of Benjamin (mix of Hawk and vampire-half-blood)
- **Jovi:** son of Bastien and Victoria (half werewolf/half human)
- **Phoenix:** son of Hazel and Tejus (sentry)
- **Serena:** daughter of Hazel and Tejus (sentry)
- **Vita:** daughter of Grace and Lawrence (part-fae/human)

VITA

"It means the last Daughter of Eritopia is about to wake up."

Draven's words echoed in my head as I tried to process the information. My mind felt clouded, like someone had pressed the pause button on the flow of time.

Phoenix had plunged a knife into his chest beneath the magnolia tree.

The earth had swallowed him whole.

The magnolia blossoms were swollen red, making the tree's crown look bigger and creepily beautiful.

And we all stood there, half of us exhausted from trying to dig Phoenix from the impossible ground, and all of us stunned at the sight of the tree.

My heart broke for Serena, who was using her True Sight to look for Phoenix underground. Judging by her wide, glimmering eyes and gaping mouth, she saw something down there.

"What do you mean she's about to wake up?" I asked, trying to regain some control over my shattered senses.

"The magnolia tree is like a lifeline. It connects the Daughter in her chrysalis state to Eritopia itself, to nature," Draven explained. "According to little-known lore, a blood sacrifice can be made to summon a Daughter. And based on everything you've told me about what Phoenix did and the color of the magnolia blossoms, there is no other explanation. She's going to wake up soon. She's been summoned."

"I can see him," Serena wheezed. "He's down there with her."

"Is he okay?" I asked, my voice trembling.

"I…I'm not sure," Serena replied, squinting. "He's inside a shell, curled up next to the Daughter. There are these red veins lining the inside of the shell. They pulsate with light in regular intervals, like a heartbeat. But Phoenix isn't moving."

"That shell does more than just host the Daughter," Draven said.

"I don't care about the stupid shell right now, Draven. I care about my brother," Serena snapped. "I can see him. I can see his chest move! He's alive! But I don't know how to get to him. We need to get him out of there!"

"It's out of our hands now, Serena." Draven maintained his composure.

I tried to mirror Draven, taking comfort in the fact that Phoenix was still alive, according to Serena. I stood unsteadily. My knees quivered, but I managed to keep myself upright. Aida joined me.

I felt weak, my soul tattered and worn out. I took deep breaths and attempted to focus on something, anything that would keep me standing. I looked around and found Bijarki's steely blue gaze fixed on me.

I held it, and the view before me came into full focus.

The incubus seemed to be a sort of anchor for my shattered concentration. I tried to clear my mind, while his silver-blue irises held me steady.

He didn't have to say anything. He didn't even have to move. All I needed was his gaze attached to mine, and I found that I could again form a coherent thought and step away from the verge of collapse.

SERENA

Hansa's groans at the sight of her dead sisters still rang in my ears. I could still see the succubus nurse ending the misery of the last scout, before the Destroyers' poison forced her to die a more painful death.

Despite all that, I'd returned to the mansion with a smile tugging at the corner of my mouth, still tasting Draven's lips on mine after our kiss, and still seeing snippets of life through his eyes from our mind-meld.

Now, however, all of that felt like a thousand years ago as I probed the ground under the magnolia tree with my True Sight and watched my brother. My stomach twisted in knots, and my eyes burned from all the tears I'd shed. My hands hurt from the shovel I'd used to try to dig him out. The earth didn't want to let go of him.

He lay inside a shell of a most peculiar pearlescent pink, crossed by red veins that thickened and glowed, as if the Daughter drew some kind of energy from the magnolia tree through its roots. Phoenix was curled up in a fetal position. His chest rose slowly with each breath. He was still alive.

Whatever he's doing down there can be fixed. I can get him back.

I was transfixed by the scene, because, if not dead, Phoenix seemed to be sleeping next to the last Daughter of Eritopia. Her hand rested on his chest, and her skin was so pale it was almost white. Her long, flowing hair was a violent reddish pink.

"Draven," I said, "these red veins from the shell, they seem to converge into her back. I'm guessing she's being fed through the spine?"

Everyone else was silent around us. I couldn't look at anyone. All I could do was focus on my brother and not let him out of my True Sight. My heart thumped in my chest. Adrenaline still rushed through me.

The frustration with not being able to do more ate away at me and gnawed at my heart. Anger bubbled up.

"The shell is her egg. It's how the Daughters come to life. I reckon the veins are like feeding tubes for her, connecting her directly to Eritopia. Is she moving?" Draven asked.

"No. She seems to be asleep. Same with Phoenix. What do we do?" I asked, forcing my voice to stay even.

"Digging obviously doesn't work," Field interjected. "Do we wait?"

"Wait for what?" My tone was sharper than I'd intended.

There was no answer, and I felt the last ounces of patience seeping out of my body. Exhaustion seeped through my legs and arms, and my eyelids felt heavy. I blinked hard. I needed Phoenix up here with me. I needed my brother back.

"I don't think we can do anything other than wait," came Draven's reply.

I shook my head, unwilling to accept that as an option.

"We have to figure something out. Don't you have some Druid magic for this? You can travel between stars. Can't you get my brother back?"

"It doesn't work like that, Serena," he replied. "I'm sorry. She's keeping him there for a reason. On the bright side, he is still alive after jamming a knife into his chest. Maybe she's healing him inside that shell. Maybe they're best left alone until the Daughter wakes up."

"And when will that be?" My voice trembled as I looked at Draven.

He lowered his head. He seemed to sense that I was on edge and didn't want to push me further.

To be honest, any answer would have been a wrong answer— unless it involved pulling my brother out of the ground right then and there.

I took a deep breath and refocused on Phoenix. The moment of silence seemed to stretch forever as I watched him inhale, exhale, inhale, exhale…

The deep red veins snapped from their organic link to the magnolia tree's roots. The egg started to move upward.

I froze.

The dark brown earth was pushing the egg to the surface.

I took a few steps back and shook my head, snapping out of my True Sight. "Something's happening," I said.

The earth rumbled beneath us.

The grass trembled. Chunks of dirt sprayed up as the Daughter's egg rose out of the ground.

Aida and Vita gasped.

"What the hell?!" Jovi yelped.

The red veins were still connected to the ground, as if drawing the last remnants of energy from the dirt. They pulsed with a pinkish light. The shell shimmered in the sun and reflected the blue sky from its smooth surface.

My brother's inside.

"What's happening?" Draven asked.

"The egg. It rose up from the ground. It's here," Bijarki replied, his voice husky and low.

My instincts kicked in. My mind focused solely on getting Phoenix out of there.

"Nobody touch—"

I swung the shovel from my side with all my might and smashed the egg with one blow.

The shell popped open in large pieces, and the veins swiftly withered into thin black lines. The light inside faded. Phoenix and the Daughter faced one another with their eyes closed. Neither of them moved.

"What…what did you do?" Draven's voice was a whisper.

My brother's safety triggered the most primal of my senses. I ignored the Druid and fell to my knees.

"Phoenix!" I shouted.

I pulled the egg shells apart in order to reach him.

Field and Jovi ran up to us and helped pull him out. They laid him on the soft grass next to me.

I checked his pulse. He was alive.

"Phoenix, wake up," I said. Tears welled in my eyes.

I had very little energy left but I wanted to use it to syphon off any pain he was feeling. I closed my eyes and reached out to the small mass of scarlet red that swirled inside his chest. My palms rested on his pectorals as I drew his pain into me.

"What's going on?" Draven's voice boomed through the darkness that enveloped me and pulled me back into consciousness.

I slumped over.

Jovi held me upright while I processed the pain, allowing it to spread through my body. My head fell back, resting against Jovi's shoulder.

And then I heard the most wonderful sound—Phoenix groaning as he awoke.

I looked at him and recognized his befuddlement. He didn't know what had happened or what he was doing there.

"It's okay, Phoenix… You'll be okay," I said to him, my voice weak. Relief washed over me.

Anjani and Bijarki knelt in front of the Daughter, removing the broken shell pieces from her alabaster skin. She wheezed her first breath and sat up, big violet eyes staring at us with panic and confusion.

"The Daughter!" Bijarki exclaimed. "She's awake!"

The girl was petite. Her long, reddish pink hair covered most of her naked body like a layer of silk. She looked around with quick head turns until her eyes settled on Phoenix. A spark of recognition flickered over her face, and she immediately moved to wrap herself around him.

"Somebody get me a blanket. We need to cover her up!" Anjani barked the order to no one in particular.

Field nodded and darted inside the house to fetch covers for the Daughter. He emerged less than a minute later with a pale yellow tablecloth that he'd probably snatched from the banquet hall. Anjani tried to wrap it around the Daughter, but the girl hissed and bared her teeth at the succubus, then nuzzled her face against Phoenix's chest, which only had a faint pink scar where I guessed he'd stabbed himself.

Draven listened carefully, seemingly trying to ascertain what was going on. He called out to Bijarki, who moved next to him and described the scene in a rapid succession of muttered words I barely understood from my distance.

"You shouldn't have done that, Serena," Draven said to me, his voice somber and reprimanding.

I caressed Phoenix's face with the back of my hand but pulled it away as soon as the Daughter started hissing at me. Whatever the noise was, it sounded threatening, and I had very little strength left to defend myself. Jovi supported most of my weight.

"It's my brother, Draven. I couldn't help it," I replied.

Deep down I sensed he was right. I had rushed into it. I had given the last Daughter of Eritopia a very rude awakening, and chances were good that there would be repercussions. But as Phoenix looked at me and smiled with all the brotherly love he could muster, I knew that those repercussions could wait another day.

Draven gripped Bijarki's arm as he approached us. The Druid dropped down to his knees, carefully listening for something.

The Daughter eyed us with a mix of curiosity and suspicion, the side of her face glued to Phoenix's chest.

I caught my brother's gaze again and noticed a faint twinkle in his eyes.

"Are you okay?" I asked him.

He nodded in response.

"Do you know what happened?" I asked.

"Not really. Everything's a little fuzzy," he said, then looked down at the Daughter.

I knew my brother well enough to recognize the expression he wore. Beneath the confusion, there was fascination, perhaps even affection, aimed at the Daughter. It only made me want to ask more questions. There was clearly something going on there that none of us could properly explain.

"I can't hear her heartbeat," Draven concluded, referring to the Daughter.

"She's definitely alive," Anjani remarked. She still held the tablecloth. "She's just not very friendly right now."

"Maybe she doesn't know what's going on." Jovi didn't take his eyes off the Daughter.

"Can you hear us?" Draven addressed the Daughter.

She threw him a glance, then looked up at Phoenix.

"I think she can, but she's not interested in responding. She's interested in Phoenix," Anjani concluded, her golden-green eyes scanning the creature from head to toe. A shadow of amusement passed over her face.

Phoenix looked down at the Daughter and shifted his weight on one arm, using the other to hold her. She pulled herself closer into him, and I couldn't help but cock my head as I watched the scene unfold before me.

"You're the one who gave her the blood sacrifice," the Druid told Phoenix. "I think she may talk to you. Say something."

"What am I supposed to say?"

My brother was a notorious charmer when it came to girls, making this entire situation even more intriguing. If he couldn't find any words to say to the Daughter, then she must possess some great power. She looked at him with warmth, as if fully trusting him.

Anjani handed him the cloth in slow motion.

The Daughter looked over her shoulder and hissed at her.

The succubus raised her hands in a peaceful gesture. From what I could tell, even in her newborn nakedness, the Daughter instilled fear in Eritopians.

"Cover her up, and see how she reacts," Anjani told Phoenix.

He nodded and moved to wrap the Daughter in the tablecloth. Much to our surprise, she allowed him to cover her. She carefully watched as he pulled the fabric over her shoulders.

"Are you okay?" he asked her gently.

She didn't answer, but her violet eyes glimmered slightly, her gaze locked with his. He gave her a reassuring smile, and his hands rested on her arms.

"You're safe here with us, you know. The Druid has been looking after you for a very long time," Phoenix continued.

The Daughter's gaze shifted to Draven again, who waited quietly on his knees.

"Does she have a name?" I asked and immediately regretted it as she moved her attention to me.

The gravity of my previous actions started to weigh heavily on me, slumping my shoulders and slowing my breath. I was in some kind of trouble. It felt like trouble. But then again, she seemed to be suspicious and aggressive toward anyone who wasn't Phoenix, not just me.

"What's your name?" Phoenix asked her.

A moment passed before she let a heavy sigh roll out of her chest.

"I don't know," she answered.

My jaw dropped. She could speak. I looked around and saw my expression mirrored on my friends' faces. No one moved, except for Phoenix, who looked surprisingly comfortable so close to the Daughter.

"How are you feeling?" he asked.

"I don't know."

"What *do* you know?"

She frowned, her lips tightened, and she seemed to struggle internally.

"Nothing," she told Phoenix. "I don't know my name. I don't know what I'm doing here. I only know what I feel, and I feel *you*."

"Does she know *what* she is?" Draven asked as he stood up.

"Do you know the Daughters of Eritopia?" Phoenix squeezed her shoulders gently.

She shook her head.

"What's Eritopia?"

At that point, my weakened synapses were able to put two and two together. She'd been connected to the very nature of Eritopia through that egg. I'd broken her out of her sleep without letting whatever process she was going through end on its own.

Phoenix didn't give up. "Do you know where you come from?"

She shook her head again.

"I don't know anything. I don't…I don't even know your name," the Daughter replied, tears glazing her eyes.

"I'm Phoenix," he smiled softly and pointed at me. "That's my sister, Serena."

She looked at me again, and I wanted to disappear before she decided that I wasn't worthy of life. But she didn't say anything.

I took it as a positive sign that she didn't hiss at me again.

I had no idea what she was thinking, and, given how confused she was, she probably didn't know what power she held or how destructive she could be. How could I trust her not to smite me on a simple whim?

"This is what I meant, Serena." Draven's voice shot through me. "She was still in the egg. The process was supposed to end naturally. She was going to hatch in her own time. Because of her premature birth, she's most likely confused, lacking crucial knowledge."

Leave it to the Druid to make me feel like the worst person in Eritopia. Besides Azazel, of course. No one could top him.

I took a deep breath and held my chin up.

"I'm sorry, Draven," I said. "As I told you, I reacted on instinct."

"And you damaged the last Daughter of Eritopia," came his reply, biting into my core.

But I was too tired to argue. Too weak to do anything, really. I had no choice but to let him reprimand me. I deserved it, after all.

"What do we do now?" I asked, trying to change the subject and move the focus from my misdemeanor to a solution.

"There isn't much we can do right now, other than take care of her and hope her knowledge soon rises to the surface," Draven replied.

I looked at the Daughter again and couldn't help but notice how fragile she seemed in my brother's arms.

She had incredible powers, and she could probably be as cruel and as terrifying as her sisters, yet in that moment she seemed so lost. No wonder she held on to Phoenix—he was the only creature she had ever been close to after all that time spent in an egg.

AidA

Time seemed to finally slow down for me. Judging by the dim lights in their eyes, it had slowed for Field and Vita as well. To say that we were exhausted was an understatement. My whole body ached, and my palms were sore from the insane amount of shoveling we'd attempted against an earth that didn't want us anywhere near Phoenix.

Nevertheless, watching him alive and conscious on the grass and holding the last Daughter of Eritopia in his arms had made the previous horror and grief subside. After the ravaging adrenaline rush, after the crying and struggling to get him out of the ground, after hoping he might still be alive, it was good to see him intact, despite all the confusion.

My attention shifted to the Daughter, who didn't strike me as the all-powerful creature previously described by Draven. She looked small and scared, not knowing where or who she was. I couldn't help but feel sorry for her—I could only imagine what it felt like for her to wake up for the first time surrounded by complete strangers and with no knowledge of her purpose in life.

"She is most likely as powerful as her sisters," Draven said.

Phoenix stood up and brought her up with him. They both staggered but leaned into each other until they could hold their own.

"But without her knowledge, she might lack control and pretty much kill us all," the Druid continued.

Leave it to the Druid to be the cold shower to my joy of seeing everyone alive and well. I suddenly became aware of exactly how dangerous the pale girl with reddish pink hair and violet eyes could be.

"Oh wow, way to bury the lead there!" I remarked sarcastically.

"I'm merely stating the facts. You can channel your discontent on your friend, Serena, since she's the cause of this mess," he replied.

I instantly looked at Serena and was surprised to see her quiet with her gaze on her brother. She didn't seem to hear Draven, and I figured she was too busy feeling relief at the sight of Phoenix walking and talking.

In other circumstances, I would've agreed that she'd acted without thinking, but I couldn't help but put myself in her shoes.

If I'd known Jovi was inside that egg, I would have done the same. Blood was thicker than rational thought sometimes.

"Phoenix, what do you remember?" I asked, hoping to move the conversation along. I was in no mood to hear Serena get reprimanded for being a good sister.

Phoenix scratched the back of his head and looked down at the scar on his chest. The Daughter's fingers brushed over it gently, tracing the short line up and down.

"I honestly don't know how to explain it all," he replied.

"Well, how about you try?" I felt a whiff of irritation tickling my spine. "If not for yourself, maybe for us, since we've been digging for hours, trying to get you out after you stabbed yourself. You know us, right? Your friends?"

An awkward silence ensued. Phoenix turned to face me, then looked at Field and Vita and the shovels at our feet. He frowned and bit his lower lip, then gave me his most genuine set of puppy eyes.

"I am so sorry, Aida. I'm sorry, guys," he said. "I had no control over what I was doing. I felt like I was in a dream. A couple of nights ago, after we met the Daughters, I had a dream about them. They gave me a knife and told me that I was the only one who could awaken their sister. Thing is, when I woke up, I actually had that knife in my hand. It was old and made of stone. It was real. I carried it with me, trying to figure out what it was for and how to do whatever it was I had to do. I wanted to tell you guys, but I didn't know how to. All I could think of was getting the Daughter out of the egg. I guess I felt some kind of connection to her."

He looked at the Daughter and smiled, and she mirrored his expression with a violet glimmer in her eyes and rested her head against his chest.

Connection is the understatement of the day.

"Then we fought those shape-shifters to rescue a woman, and I think I got hurt, because I blacked out," Phoenix continued.

Anjani bowed before him with gratitude.

He didn't seem to recognize her, but that didn't come as a surprise. He'd banged his head pretty hard.

"And for that, I am in your debt," the succubus replied.

Phoenix's face lit up as he looked at her, then at Jovi, and he smiled with delight. "Good to see we all made it out of there after all," he said.

"Yeah, Field swooped in and saved your ass," I shot back, still a little mad.

We'd all been through so much to protect Phoenix, save him, and keep him alive. To hear him sound so capricious about it… But in all fairness, he'd been a good friend, almost getting himself killed to save Jovi and a complete stranger. I had to push harder and get my emotions under control. I had to at least give Phoenix a chance to tell us the whole story.

He looked at Field, nodded his thank you, and glanced at the Daughter again.

"After that, it was all like a dream. I saw her down there in her egg. I kept hearing the Daughters telling me that I had to sacrifice my own blood to bring her to life. I couldn't bear the thought of her stuck in that shell, shut off from everything. I don't even remember waking up, really. I got out of bed, and I went to the garden, knife in hand. It was automatic, like my brain had no control over my body. I drove the knife into my chest, and I wanted to scream and shout, but I was powerless. Then it all faded away. And I woke up here, with you guys," Phoenix concluded.

It took us all some time to process everything.

I connected the dots in my mind, wondering about the connection he said he'd felt with the Daughter. Looking at them now, it made sense. He'd basically sacrificed himself for her. And even in her slumber, she probably didn't want him to die, so she'd sucked him into the shell with her.

My guess was that she'd kept him there and healed him, as if her consciousness had transcended her body. Her power seemed spectacular from that angle alone. What she was capable of, however, seemed like a distant idea compared to her current state.

She'd been pulled out of her shell instead of being allowed to hatch. No wonder she was confused. And yet, she seemed so affected by Phoenix, so tied to him, as if he was the only creature in the world. They'd shared an egg together, after all. It was a fascinating thing to observe—this unexpected relationship between them.

As I watched them, I noticed her affectionate gestures toward him, as if Phoenix were her protector and the only one she trusted.

The memory of last night crept back to me.

I sensed Field standing next to me for the first time in hours. We'd been so brutally broken out of our moment when Vita's screams pierced through the mansion that we hadn't had a chance to process everything.

Now that the tragedy had subsided, and we were all back together, I remembered everything. My stomach churned, recalling how close our faces had been, how his lips had parted, inches from mine. What *had* happened, really? What had he been thinking? What was he going to do?

I looked at Field and was surprised to find his gaze on me. Shadows fluttered over his turquoise eyes, his expression firm and unreadable. For the length of a lazy second I wished I'd had Serena's sentry abilities, so I could look into his mind and understand what was going through his head.

I had a feeling he was thinking about the same thing. His gaze softened. I wanted to say something.

The back of his hand brushed against mine, and billions of little electrical currents ran through me, forcing me to take a deep breath in order to maintain some form of control over my senses.

I realized that whatever had happened between us in the basement had been real, but it was completely unexpected, and I didn't know how to react—a predicament I'd been getting myself into quite frequently since we'd arrived in Eritopia.

He'd gotten so close to me that I could hear the wall I'd meticulously built around myself crumble piece by piece, as I stared into his greenish-blue eyes. Something had changed dramatically in our dynamic, and I wasn't sure how I was going to deal with it, or where it would lead.

With all the madness around us, I wondered if I needed this one thing to stay the same. I wondered if I ought to keep the wall from crumbling.

But there was a trace of hope blossoming inside my heart, whispering ideas that I had abandoned long ago about Field. One by one, thoughts of something intense and incredibly meaningful started to bubble up to the surface—forgotten desires and feelings that only Field could untangle.

JOVI

The horror of losing Phoenix had finally dimmed to a mild ache in my stomach. Everything had happened so quickly and unexpectedly that I didn't have time to process each moment properly. My internal systems were slowing down, signaling the need for food and rest so that I could wrap my head around it all.

I stood motionless next to Anjani, Vita, Field and Aida. I watched Draven, Bijarki, and Serena talk about what we were going to do next, giving Anjani the occasional sideways glance when she wasn't looking. Her skin had this beautiful shimmer in the sunshine, and I had a hard time looking away.

My attention alternated between the succubus and the Daughter. I feared that the new Daughter would be as cruel as her sisters. Yet she seemed nothing like the goddesses we'd met the other day, with masks made of gold and no words of comfort for those in need of help.

This Daughter was fragile and confused, nestled in Phoenix's arms, and wrapped up in an old tablecloth. I couldn't imagine seeing her under one of those masks, killing a man with a simple touch, or robbing him of his eyesight.

"What do we do now?" I asked.

The wolf in me picked up Anjani's spicy scent. Heat spread through my chest. I held on to her aroma as an anchor, keeping me on my feet. I only partially focused on our next steps. My mind preoccupied itself with getting closer to the inherently seductive creature next to me.

"The Oracles need to eat and rest for the day," Draven replied. "They must recover and prepare for tomorrow."

"What's happening tomorrow?" Aida looked pale, leaning against Field.

"You need to tap into your visions. It's our best chance to defeat Azazel. Kristos's father has joined his ranks, and we've lost any potential support from the incubi at this point in time," Draven explained.

My sister didn't seem happy with the prospect of more visions, though I couldn't blame her—she didn't ask for this. She'd spent her whole life learning and training to join GASP to become a guardian of Earth and a maintainer of peace, not to become a pawn in a bloody war in the In-Between.

Vita looked equally drained.

Phoenix focused on the Daughter. I wasn't sure if he was even listening to Draven.

"The Red Tribe will fight with us. We've managed to secure that alliance," the Druid continued. "They're going to reach out to the Dearghs, the Lamias, and the Sluaghs, though I'm not crossing my fingers for the latter."

"Why do you say that?" Serena asked him.

"The Sluaghs have been thriving with Azazel's war. They're generally wretched creatures, parasites who inhabit the bodies of the recently deceased. And there have been so many of them lately that the Sluagh population is increasing every day. On one hand, their numbers are useful, but I'm not sure they'd be interested in biting the hand that inadvertently feeds them."

"What's our end game here, though?" Field replied.

I noticed his arm wrapping around my sister's shoulders. I wasn't sure what to think of it, but knowing my sister, there probably was a little wolf-girl inside of her dancing around with glee. I decided I'd worry about them later. I had trouble focusing with the succubus just inches away from me.

"We can't rely on the incubi to fight Azazel, which is a major problem since they represent the highest percentage of Eritopia's population," Draven explained. "But there are many other species that call this world home, and they all stand to lose everything if Azazel wins. We have to gather as many of them as we can and forge an alliance. Along with the Oracles and the Daughter.

Despite her current condition, it's our best shot to destroy him."

"Speaking of which, I'd like to get her inside to rest, if you don't mind," Phoenix replied, while the Daughter stood motionless in his arms.

Draven nodded his approval, and Phoenix took her inside the mansion. It was so good to see him walking and talking again. I couldn't help but smile. I caught a glimpse of Anjani out the corner of my eye; she'd been watching me but instantly looked away when my gaze met hers.

My sister wasn't too steady on her feet, but Field held her up with concern etched into his sharp features.

"Field, can you take Aida inside, please?" I asked him. "She needs food and rest."

He nodded and helped her into the house. My heart twisted at the sight of her being so soft and weak, but I took comfort in the fact that she was in good hands with the Hawk. Aida would be up and running circles around us by morning, for sure.

I figured it was a good time to take my leave as well, but I wasn't interested in being on my own. I brushed Anjani's arm with the back of my hand, and she looked at me with wide golden-green eyes.

"Let me show you around. You can wash up, eat, and rest a little. You've dealt with enough for one morning," I told her.

I'd expected her to contradict me and put on her warrior chick bravado, but she didn't. Instead, she nodded and followed me inside.

There was a spare bedroom next to mine upstairs, so I decided to take her there. It seemed like a girl's room with soft pinks and yellows on the wallpaper and delicate floral patterns on the bed covers. The windows were tall, and there was a set of narrow French doors opening out to a small terrace facing south.

I showed Anjani to the ensuite bathroom and sat down in one of the two armchairs facing the bed. I heard the lock turn on the door and the water run into the tub. I wasn't ready to leave yet. I wanted to make sure that she had everything she needed when she came out.

I let my feet rest for about five minutes, then started rummaging through the dresser for some clothes. I picked out a white gown, which, judging by its era of manufacture, was most likely intended as an undergarment for those fancy summer dresses that women wore on southern cotton plantations. I figured she could do with a change of clothes, at least for a day. I also wanted to see how that fine white organza would look on her body, hugging her breasts and round hips.

I heard the door open, and I turned around to show her the gown.

I froze.

My heart stopped.

The air left my lungs.

I watched Anjani in her full naked splendor walk out of the bathroom. She stilled. Her muscles tensed in her thighs. Her eyes widened. Water trickled down her silvery skin and set my soul on fire.

I wanted to look away. I tried. But I couldn't take my eyes off her.

Every curve, every line, every bit of her was designed to drive a man like me mad, to enslave me and consume me while I welcomed it with arms wide open.

My inner-wolf howled like a maniac, as if Anjani was the full moon that guided my entire existence. Judging by the stunned look on her face, she probably thought she'd walk out to an empty room after her shower.

"What…what are you doing here?" she asked with a hiss.

"I…I wanted to make sure you had everything you needed here." My voice was barely audible.

Anjani's skin lit up with a familiar glow, the one I'd seen the night before in our tent. She was blushing in her succubus way. My core burned with delight, and I shifted from one leg to the other to relieve some of the tension gathered below my waist.

"I'm sorry," I managed to say and used every ounce of strength I had in me to look away. I held out the gown for her. "I found this. Thought you could use it."

"What's that?" she asked. Every second she stood there naked prolonged my agony. I forced myself to look away when all I wanted was to take it all in.

"Just a dress. Figured you needed some fresh clothes."

"I didn't realize you'd still be here," Anjani said, her tone slicing through me like a knife, making me feel like the ultimate perv.

She pulled the floral pattern cover from the bed and wrapped herself in it. She would've had to move and reach out in order to get the gown from me, and I wasn't willing to risk taking a step toward her. I was aroused and terrified at the same time.

"This is your room, you can rest here," I said. I left the gown on the bed between us and moved to the door.

"Jovi." Anjani's voice stopped me as my foot reached the threshold.

I looked over my shoulder, and our eyes met.

"Thank you for everything," she said.

It felt like some sort of concession coming from her, as if she'd lowered her defenses enough to acknowledge me as more than just a chunk of meat. I wasn't sure what she was thanking me for, but given her past experiences growing up in the wild and being taught to rely only on herself, I figured she'd finally decided to welcome my support.

She probably wasn't used to hospitality, to being looked after by a man. She didn't seem mad about my presence there. My intentions had been pure, after all. Not my fault she didn't know the concept of towels.

I smiled, nodded, and left.

Another minute with her, and I probably would have had to pick a fight with that bed cover.

Phoenix

I showed the Daughter around the mansion. We passed through the banquet hall, Draven's studio, and the library. I showed her to the girls' bedroom upstairs, where I picked out a simple summer dress for her to wear—a white cotton gown with delicate lace details around the neck and sleeves.

She dropped the tablecloth to the floor, and I instinctively turned around. I had a feeling that if I got a good look at her, I would never be able to part from her again. And despite my attachment to her, there was a part of me that didn't want to be so vulnerable. I stilled, waiting for the fabric to stop rustling.

The dress fit her perfectly, with a rounded neckline and three-quarter sleeves with lace frills. The fabric hugged her tiny waist perfectly and expanded into a wide skirt all the way down to her ankles. While her pale skin competed with the whiteness of the fabric, her hair cascaded in fiery contrast over her shoulders.

I had to move. I had to get her out of there before my mind drifted in an inappropriate direction. We toured the top floor and then went back downstairs, where we found a beautiful tea room hidden behind the dining hall, complete with Baroque oil paintings and gilded details on the classical furniture.

She didn't seem to like the indoors much, and soon enough we found ourselves wandering toward the back garden. She was fascinated by the greenhouse in particular, and we spent some time there.

It was hot and humid, but I couldn't bring myself to suggest going elsewhere. Something inside of me pulled me closer to this creature I knew nothing about. I had never spent so much time or energy focused on someone the way I did with her.

It felt strange but simultaneously exhilarating. Every time she looked at me, my heart stopped for a moment, then resumed its thunderous beating against my ribcage. I'd done the craziest thing for her, nearly killing myself. I'd had no control over my body or my senses. In any other circumstances, I would've berated myself.

But watching her as she strolled through the greenhouse, sniffing the abundance of weirdly beautiful plants and flowers, crinkling her nose when she got a whiff of a foul-smelling herb, and smiling when she discovered a bright purple blossom that resembled an iris, I couldn't help but feel like it had all been worth it.

She was awake and out of that shell, able to breathe and experience everything like the rest of us. On top of that, she was the most incredible creature I had ever laid eyes on—small but gorgeous with gentle curves, hair the color of an autumn sunset, and curious violet eyes that never stopped exploring and analyzing.

Every time her gaze met mine, fire burned through my stomach and paralyzed my senses. Her lips were soft and full, almost begging to be kissed. And when they stretched into a smile and revealed two rows of pearly white teeth, I melted.

I smiled back and wiped a bead of sweat from my brow. "I take it you like it in here."

She nodded and shifted her focus back on the purple flower. Her delicate fingers gently traced the contours of each petal.

"It's so beautiful," she whispered.

Nowhere near as beautiful as you. I took a deep breath, trying to keep myself cool and composed. I felt like I had to make a good impression and show her my truth, our truth, about this world. With all its faults and cruelty, Eritopia was a good place and worthy of salvation. It felt like my job to make her see that.

After all, she had the power to make it better or break it forever.

"I understand that the whole of Eritopia is like this," I said, "filled with fascinating flora and home to intriguing creatures—so different from my people back home."

"You're not from here?" she asked, a questioning look on her beautiful face.

"No." I shook my head and smiled. "Eritopia is part of what we call the In-Between, which is a space we pass through when we travel via portal from our world, Earth, to the supernatural dimension, where many of us have roots. This is the first time I've been to the In-Between for this long and my first time in Eritopia. I would've never imagined Eritopia even existed, otherwise."

"How did you come here? Why did you come here?"

I liked her curiosity. It gave me a chance to tell her our side of the story. As drawn as I was to her, there was still a part of me that pushed me to use a strategic approach and think of the long-term and her influence on her sisters.

"The Druid brought us here with his magic. My friends and I had gone to a fae celebration in another galaxy and suddenly found ourselves here. Aida, myself, and Vita were told that we are Oracles and that we have the ability to see the past, the present, and the future of everything. We obviously didn't believe him at first." I chuckled, remembering my confusion during our first days here.

She cocked her head, listening as I told her about the Nevertide Oracle who had passed her powers to our mothers eighteen years ago, about the visions we'd had so far, and about Azazel's reign of terror.

"I think Bijarki and Draven can tell you more about the Destroyers. I'm not nearly informed enough on this subject. All I know is that they cause pain and suffering and kill without mercy. There's no place for them in this world. In any world, for that matter." I heaved a sigh.

Her eyebrows drew into a frown, passing shadows across her face, and she walked toward me, hands at her sides. As she closed the distance between us, I felt my breath falter and my heart drum frenetically. The more time I spent around her, the more I was torn between mindless attraction and respectful reverence.

"You don't like Azazel," the Daughter said slowly as she stopped inches from me.

"I don't think anyone likes Azazel. I'm guessing the only one who likes Azazel is Azazel," I quipped, trying to relieve some of the tension I felt lingering in the back of my neck.

"I don't like him either," she replied. "I don't like him because he makes you sad."

Her candor was disarming, and I couldn't help but smile.

"That's okay. I'm not that bothered since you're here now," I said to her, drawing my face closer to hers.

My eyes felt locked on hers, and I had the impression of sinking in two pools of vibrant violet, the unknown of her very being pulling me deeper and deeper. She didn't move, didn't say a word; instead she held my gaze, and I suddenly found myself wondering what she was thinking.

I was tempted to try a mind-meld, but the rattling above us broke my train of thought. I looked up and saw the rain tapping against the glass panes of the greenhouse and pouring down the sides. The skies were covered with gray clouds being pushed by a strong wind. Lightning flashed in jagged lines.

"What's that?" she asked, looking up.

"That's rain. Water pours down from the sky sometimes and nurtures the land."

"Rain," she said, letting the word roll off her tongue. "Rain gives life."

She smiled and darted outside before I could stop her. She pushed the glass door open and ran into the garden out back. Magnolia trees bordered the property in shades of pink and white, trembling beneath the rainfall. Petals dropped to the ground here and there. The wind whistled overhead as the rain intensified, rapping against the soft grass.

I ran outside to find the Daughter laughing. She stood in the middle of the garden with her arms stretched out, happy to receive every single drop that the sky had to give her. It darkened her hair to a gloomy pink. Water trickled over her lips.

I watched her as she spun in the rain enjoying a natural occurrence that drove most of us to shelter. The water soon soaked her dress. The material clung to her curves in a way that made my temperature rise. I didn't want to move. I didn't want to disturb her—she looked so happy and alive.

She sneezed.

The noise surprised her, and she laughed. Then she sneezed again and laughed even harder. I laughed as well, watching a Daughter of Eritopia in the rain. But then the sneezing grew more intense, and she stopped laughing and moving.

My own nose itched all of a sudden, and my eyes burned.

I reached her in several steps and noticed her red nose and teary eyes as she tried to wipe the water from her face. Steam drifted out of her shivering body, and I realized that I had to get her inside and warmed up fast before she came down with a cold or worse. I was taken aback by how quickly her symptoms had come on.

I took her in my arms and carried her inside. She was silent, tender against my chest, trembling and sniffing. I raced up the stairs and went straight into my room, placing my little bundle of pink hair and soft white flesh on the bed. I retrieved several large towels from the bathroom, and wrapped her in them.

I used one to dry her hair, and she silently sat there watching me for a while, the faint shadow of a smile flickering on her lips. Soon enough, her eyes closed, and I laid her on one side of the bed. I pulled the bed cover over her as she drifted off to sleep.

She seemed content, covered in warm linens and towels. The rain outside stopped, and the clouds broke apart. The sun shone and threw warm rays into my room. I pulled a chair close to the bed and sat there, watching her while she slept.

Her body moved with every breath she took, and her dark red brows furrowed slightly once in a while. Was she dreaming?

I couldn't bring myself to leave her, and the thought startled me.

What had she done to me? How had I become so tied to this gorgeous creature?

And why was I so okay with it?

AiDA

I leaned against Field as we walked into the banquet hall, where breakfast was still being served—although at this hour it could easily be considered brunch. We didn't care. We were famished.

We ate in silence, sitting next to each other, and my mind rocked back and forth, oscillating between last night's moment with Field and everything that came afterward, including the forced hatching of the last Daughter. The latter had definitely made it onto my "top five weirdest moments in Eritopia" list. It didn't beat the flickering runes I'd seen on my body the other night, but it was a decent contender for the upper echelon of freaky occurrences.

Field's presence so close to me soon started to have a dominant effect. I found myself giving him sideways glances and wondering what he was thinking about. The silence shifted from normal to awkward, as we both slowed down and picked at the pancakes on our plates and sipped our coffee.

"Field," I said.

He looked at me, his turquoise eyes lighting up as soon as they met mine.

"I want to thank you," I continued, my voice lower than usual.

"For what?"

"For everything. For everything you've done, for being here, for being an amazing friend. We're so lucky to have you around." I was exhausted, judging by my mild slur and dim tone.

Despite the nourishment, what I needed most was sleep. Long hours of it, uninterrupted. I noticed a frown pass over Field's face, and I wasn't sure what to make of it, especially when he shifted his gaze to his plate.

"I'm still trying to wrap my head around Phoenix and the Daughter," came his completely unrelated reply. "It's so good to see him alive, but at the same time I can't quite put my finger on this connection he seems to have with the Daughter. It's like they've become inseparable."

"Yeah, me neither." I nodded slowly. "It might have started from his vision of her from the past, sleeping in her shell. And if the Daughters picked up on that and gave him that knife, clearly this was somehow meant to happen. Though I don't understand what their end game is and why Phoenix and the Daughter seem so attached."

"We'll have to keep an eye on them going forward," Field said and gulped down the rest of his coffee.

I pushed the chair back and stood up, ready for my beauty sleep. But my legs didn't feel like obeying the rest of my body, and I wobbled, prompting Field to rise out of his chair and lift me in his arms.

While exhaustion may have finally prevailed over me, I had enough sense to marvel at the sensation of his arms around me.

Field held me, my feet dangling, as I wrapped my arms around his neck for support. I melted into his chest, tired and grateful to feel him so close. His body was hard and unforgiving, but his grip was gentle and cautious. I let my head rest on his chest as he carried me upstairs. His heartbeat drummed in my ear.

We made it to my room upstairs, and he set me back on my feet. I looked up and gave him a weak smile as a thank you and staggered into the bathroom.

"I need a shower before I can even touch that bed," I mumbled.

I locked the door behind me and leaned against it. My breathing was fast and uneven, mimicking my heart. I'd felt so safe for a brief moment in Field's arms, tucked away from the whole world and everything that wanted to kill me. I needed a few seconds to get a grip.

I turned on the water and peeled off my clothes, dumping them in an old laundry basket. I'd deal with those later. I welcomed the stream over my face and body. My muscles relaxed, and my skin was thankful for every drop. I washed my hair with soap and cleaned all the dirt away; my digging attempts had been quite messy.

I stepped out of the shower and wrapped a towel around myself, my mind wandering toward Field and what it had felt like against his body. No wonder my legs were so weak.

I twisted my hair and let it loose over one shoulder, enough to feel some cool air against the back of my neck. I wiped the mirror above the sink with my palm to get a quick look at myself. My eyes were droopy and bloodshot, but some color had returned to my cheeks thanks to the food.

My mind zoned in on the bed waiting for me on the other side of the door, and I came out of the bathroom with the sole intention of collapsing under the covers and fading out for a day or so.

I stilled at the sight of Field in one of the armchairs facing the bed. He was still there. My nakedness suddenly became my biggest problem, as only a towel stood between us. My cheeks burned, and my heart jumped into my throat and refused to back down no matter how much I swallowed.

He sprang to his feet. His eyes darkened as his gaze ran all over me, lingering here and there quietly. Our eyes met, and I felt my knees preparing for an even greater betrayal.

"I'm sorry," he said, his voice raspy and low. "I just wanted to make sure you came out of there okay. You weren't too steady on your feet."

I couldn't say anything. I wanted to say everything that was going through my mind in this moment and ask him to stay with me. But my lips were sealed, and my words were stuck somewhere in the back of my head where I couldn't reach them.

All I could do was nod, while he stood there, motionless, watching me. He took a deep breath and headed for the door, running a hand through his long black hair.

"I…I should let you sleep," he said.

He shifted his gaze to the floor, walked out, and closed the door behind him.

My legs finally gave in, and I slumped on the bed, catching my breath and clutching the corners of the towel above my chest. I lay on my back and closed my eyes, counting each inhale while the image of Field lingered in my mind. I drifted away.

Vita

I was in the dining room when the rain started pouring outside, tapping against the windows. It had taken me a while to leave the garden, and Bijarki had quietly waited on the porch steps, occasionally glancing my way, as if making sure I was okay. He kept his distance, as I'd asked before, but he stuck around. I couldn't help feeling thankful for his presence.

We ate in silence on opposite sides of the table. I occasionally looked at him, but not once did our eyes meet. When one of us looked up, the other looked away.

"How was the trip?" I eventually asked, no longer comfortable with the absence of words between us.

Bijarki's gaze rose from his place and settled on mine. A familiar warmth enveloped me, and I welcomed the feeling. After this wretched morning, it was very much needed.

"The succubi's poisoned arrows were excellent deterrents for the shape-shifters along the way," he replied and poured himself a glass of water from one of the pitchers on the table.

"What's the Red Tribe like?"

He took a deep breath before he answered, as if choosing his words carefully. The shadow of a smile passed over his face. There was a story there I didn't know, and I found myself intrigued.

"They're quite fiery," Bijarki said. "They live freely at the base of one of the northern mountains, hunting and gathering their food, enjoying everything that life has to offer without adhering to any citadel laws. I sort of envy them for it."

"For their freedom, you mean?"

He nodded, then smiled at me, setting off a fire in the pit of my stomach.

"They get to do what they want, whenever they want, and they account to no one for it. Sure, they have their rules and traditions, but they're happy and wild and make no concession. I've never been so deep inside a succubi tribe before. It was fascinating. Our society doesn't treat them kindly, and they're often ill-spoken about."

"Ill-spoken?" I asked, suddenly thinking of Anjani in a whole new light.

The warrior succubus was someone I deeply admired, and I'd expected the rest of the world to appreciate creatures like her as well.

"They're considered promiscuous, lustful, and unattached," he replied, his gaze drilling a hole straight into my soul.

I couldn't help but draw some parallels between the succubi and incubi based on what I knew and what he told me. They didn't seem so different at all.

"But lust is sort of in your nature, isn't it?"

"In a way, yes. But at the end of the day, most of the incubi adhere to stricter, monogamous rules. Most are fine with wives, which is more of a title, a contract between a male and a female. The majority of these are arranged by society; some of us search for a soulmate, a partner for life. That is a much deeper, more intense bond that transcends any piece of parchment. It focuses on the emotion, rather than the company.

"There are succubi raised in the cities, but the majority of them live in free tribes, away from the males. We only meet when it's time to reproduce and give birth to incubus heirs. Some succubi tribes have long-term agreements with neighboring cities, where they agree to mate for the purpose of continuing an incubus line. They get treated with gold and other riches in return.

"There's maybe a handful of succubi who leave their tribes to live with the males of our species out of pure love. We've been separated like this for millennia now, long before I was even born. Lust is in our genes, and it's what keeps our species going. Marriage is a contract of convenience. Love is rare and precious," Bijarki explained.

"So, you do look for love." I heard my conclusion roll off my tongue and felt myself blush when his gaze softened and his lips stretched lazily into a smile.

"Lust is common in Eritopia. Love is a foreign concept. But when it does happen, it consumes, and it takes hold of one's soul. When an incubus falls in love, it's equal parts extraordinary and painful. It's intense but worth it. At least that's what I'm told," he said slowly.

"You've never been in love?" I asked, even as I reprimanded myself for such brazen curiosity.

What am I trying to get out of him?

Bijarki tilted his head and leaned against the back of his chair, while his expression sent heatwaves in my direction.

I gripped my coffee cup and sipped quietly, unable to break eye contact. Whatever I was getting myself into with these questions, a part of me—a much bigger part of me than I wanted to admit— was very curious to find out where it would lead.

"I've never been in love, no," came his response.

I measured my breath and nodded in return, out of words and thankfully out of intimate questions to ask.

"But then again, up until a few days ago I didn't even consider the concept," Bijarki continued, prompting me to pay more attention to his elusive body language. His slow and deliberate movements were telling me something new. "I've never met anyone I could consider capable of stirring me in any way, until I laid my eyes on you."

My heart started racing again, and my fingers fiddled with the cup's delicate porcelain handle. I needed something menial to do just to keep myself together.

"You see, you fascinate me, Vita. You're a creature of contrasts, and I'm having a hard time figuring you out. That's never happened to me before. I usually look at people, and I can immediately tell what they are, what they would do in certain situations, and how I feel about them. But you? You stun me."

His words rolled out without inhibitions and crashed into me. I lowered my gaze and felt the heat rising into my throat and spreading to my cheeks. I felt naked, completely powerless before him, and yet I wanted to hear more. I needed to hear him say all those things because they all confirmed something that had been eluding definition in my mind for a while.

"I am attracted to you, yes," he said. "Despite the tragic circumstances, I can't seem to get you out of my head. Last night, the succubi wanted me. They lingered around me as we feasted around the campfire."

My heart twisted in knots at the thought of succubi seducing him, and I looked up. I got lost in his eyes, two pools of silver that flickered with distant lights, telling me a little bit more than his words.

"But I turned them all down. I couldn't get you out of my mind, not even for a second, not even with all those gorgeous creatures offering me their bodies to satisfy everything that has been burning inside of me lately. You have my full attention, young fire fae."

I was speechless, my mind blank, my fingers trembling on the cup's handle. My body softened from the heat of his unexpected candor. My breath stopped, and I found myself unable to take my eyes off him.

He sat up straight and added another pancake to his plate, eating as if nothing had happened, as if he'd just told me the weather conditions for tomorrow or something equally as trivial.

I was baffled as I combed through his statement and broke it down in my head phrase by phrase. It seemed like a confession of sorts. His words resonated deeply inside of me, and I had to figure out how I felt about that. I'd already accepted the fact that I was attracted to him. I just didn't expect him to genuinely feel the same way. What was I supposed to do with this new information?

He broke through my thoughts. "That being said, I am also aware that you're not immune to my incubus nature, and I swear to you, on everything I hold dear, that I am doing my best to keep my powers under control whenever I'm around you. If you ever come to me, it will be of your own accord, not my influence. I've promised to keep my distance from you, as you've asked. And I can assure you that my intentions are good. But you can't ask me to turn off what I feel, because I can't. I want you. And that won't change."

I was stunned. A bright fire blazed inside me, ignited by a flicker of lust. His effect over me was undeniable. I'd frequently doubted it to be genuine, choosing to blame it on his incubus nature.

Yet now he was telling me that he'd been keeping himself under control around me, leaving me to conclude once more and with even more certainty that everything I'd been feeling toward him was of my own making, something I could no longer deny or control.

I needed a few deep breaths to gather enough sense to respond to his statement.

He'd been so kind, so open and respectful, and I'd been acting like a damsel made of ice, loaded with biting remarks, and unable to admit that everything I was feeling about him was real.

"We're in this mess together, all of us," I replied, my voice barely a whisper. "We need to get along in order for this alliance to work, in order for us to defeat Azazel. You keeping your distance from me seems counter-productive at this point in time, and I see no need for it. You've been nothing but good and decent toward me. I have no reason to push you away."

His expression changed, softening into something I didn't quite recognize. I wondered if it was because it came from an incubus who had been trained for war, not feelings. He nodded in response, and I saw him relax in his chair. He smiled. His eyes darted around the room and occasionally settled on me.

I finished my meal in silence, while my body deliciously ached in his presence.

But exhaustion soon claimed me, and I excused myself. I'd deal with my reaction to Bijarki later.

I fell asleep next to Aida, my bones heavy while my heart fluttered in my chest.

Serena

I helped Draven to his room as soon as the clouds started to gather above the mansion in heavy, gray rolls.

Everyone else had scattered off to eat, shower, and sleep the events of the day off.

My mind battled with an array of thoughts and memories from the morning, unable to settle on one thing in particular.

Draven didn't say much once we got to his room. I stopped in the doorway, leaving him to walk in on his own. My intention was to leave him there, then take a long bath and sleep for an eternity.

My feet felt heavy, and my heart had sunk even deeper as I came to terms with my mistake of forcing the Daughter out of her sleep. The repercussions weren't clear just yet, other than her lack of knowledge. We didn't even know if her sisters would retaliate in any way, but the one aspect that seemed to worry me the most was the fact that I'd upset Draven. I could feel it in the tone of his voice. I'd broken something, and I felt terrible.

He moved to the bed and started unbuttoning his shirt.

My eyes followed the motions of his fingers. My throat dried up, stirring memories of our kiss and how close we'd gotten to virtually consuming each other. Reason told me to leave, but my body and my soul didn't listen.

"We'll have to do an intensive session tomorrow with the Oracles," Draven said as he removed his shirt. "I've asked Anjani to prepare some potions to help with the immersion. Time isn't on our side."

He slipped out of his boots and stilled for a moment, as if listening for something.

"What are you doing?" he asked.

"Me? N-nothing," I stuttered, breathing heavily.

I couldn't stop admiring his broad chest and massive shoulders. His rune wounds had healed almost completely, leaving behind just a few faint lines that were lighter than his tan.

"Come in. Stay here," he commanded me, a roughness in his tone that I took to mean that he was still angry with me. Every time I thought about it, I felt worse and worse.

"Why?" I asked, frustratingly unsure of myself.

I wasn't ready for another verbal pummeling over what had happened under the magnolia tree and my rash use of a shovel.

"What do you mean why?" He shot back. He sighed and changed his demeanor, as if realizing he'd sounded abrupt. "Please stay. I won't be long."

He walked into the bathroom, his fingers passing over the nearby furniture for guidance, and closed the door behind him. I stood there for a while, motionless, trying to find a way to smother the regrets that were so quick to bubble up in me.

I wanted to go back to that tent, before we'd stepped back out into the world. I wanted to get lost in his arms again, our lips and minds fused into a single sentient being that knew nothing of pain or sorrow.

Eventually I settled in the armchair where I'd slept before and stared outside the window as the rain knocked on the glass. Thunder echoed beneath the charcoal sky. I caught a glimpse of lightning here and there, zigzagging white lines disappearing in the distance. I closed my eyes for a few minutes and started mentally flipping through Draven's memories from our mind-meld again. It felt like a safe place right now.

I got a good look at his father. Draven was the spitting image of him with hair the color of sand pouring down his wide shoulders, inquisitive steel eyes, and a smooth nose. Almus had sharper edges, though, as if he'd been roughly carved into stone and brought to life, whereas Draven's face followed slightly softer lines around his temples and cheeks, with dark brown eyebrows bent in a soft arch.

I watched Draven run around in the backyard with Elissa, laughing in the sun. She looked so happy, so light and full of love.

This lonely little boy deserved all the affection she gave him and more. My stomach twisted in knots as I remembered her death through his eyes. His youth and innocence had been forever marred by that moment, reminding me of how he spoke of Eritopia when we first met. *It's cruel, and it will kill you,* he'd said. My eyes felt wet.

The bathroom door opened, startling me upright as I wiped the tears from my eyes. My grief at the thought of Draven's unimaginable pain and loneliness was quickly stuffed somewhere in the back of my head, as the sight of him wearing nothing but a towel around his narrow waist came into full view.

My senses started glitching, my eyes scanning him from head to toe, taking in every inch of wet skin and muscle beneath. I bit into my lower lip as I felt my body succumb to a series of unstoppable heatwaves. I tightened my fingers into fists in a pathetic attempt to keep my cool.

He stood there for a while, quiet and still steaming from his shower, enough for me to forget who or what I was. My mind went blank.

"There are some clean shirts and gowns in the bottom drawer here," Draven said, his finger pointing at the chest of drawers by the wall next to the bathroom door. "Pick something out and take a shower. I'm guessing you need one as much as I needed mine. I'll be waiting."

Yet another command in a rigid tone. This man was a walking, talking contradiction, and once again I felt childishly insecure around him, not knowing whether he was still upset with me or just being his usual authoritarian self.

"What…what do you mean?" I managed to ask. My throat was parched.

"I would like for you to stay here with me today."

His request was simple, yet I couldn't focus properly. My energy was at critically low levels, yet my insides burned in his proximity. My brain wasn't helping with anything.

"Why?"

"Serena, we've been through enough already," Draven replied, his voice softening. "I just want you close to me, not wandering around and out of my reach."

He baffled me, defeating my resolve with a single sentence. How could I say no to that?

I let a sigh roll out of my chest and pulled a long, white linen shirt from the bottom drawer, along with some matching, ankle-length briefs. These were men's clothes but, given they belonged in the 19th century or so, they could pass for women's attire now. Not that it mattered much in this mansion, lost in a corner of Eritopia.

I slipped into the shower and felt myself come alive under the water stream. I washed the dirt away and abused the lavender scented soap bar. When I was finally clean, I stepped out of the tub and wiped myself dry with a towel.

My mind wandered back to the Daughter. I had so many questions for her, but given her current condition, I wasn't going to get any answers. She didn't even know her own name, not to mention what her powers were and what she could do against Azazel and his horde of Destroyers. She was fragile and defenseless, and I only had myself to blame for that.

With hindsight rapidly smacking me over the head, guilt reared its ugly head again. I felt the bathroom walls closing in. I shook my head and took a few deep breaths, then slipped into the shirt and briefs, which hung loosely on me. The linen was soft and dry, and it felt good against my skin.

I came out of the bathroom to find Draven lying in bed on his side beneath the covers. He must have fallen asleep already. My mood had gone south again, and I decided there was no point in sticking around. Might as well sleep in my bed with the girls.

I moved to the door, and the floorboard creaked beneath my feet.

"Where are you going?" Draven's voice shot through the silence.

I froze, not expecting him to still be awake.

"I…I thought you were sleeping. I didn't want to bother you so I—"

"Stay. Please." He pulled the cover aside and patted the bed, inviting me to join him.

My knees softened, and I felt my temperature rise once more. Despite everything that had happened that morning, the only place I really wanted to be was that little space next to him, under a soft blanket.

"Okay. I'll just sleep in the chair. Don't worry about me," I muttered and took a few steps toward the armchair, not wanting to concede just yet. I didn't like the idea of granting him a small victory so easily.

"Serena, don't be foolish. Get in bed like a normal person. Stop trying to ruin your spine in that thing."

His tone was firm, but there was a peculiar softness underneath, which made me smile as I approached the bed. Maybe he wasn't mad at me after all, despite what my conscience was telling me. *It* clearly wasn't my friend today.

I sighed and lay down on my side, facing him, my body stiff and my heart in my throat. I swallowed it back down as Draven pulled the blanket over me, then snaked his arms around my waist and drew me closer to him.

I abandoned all my defenses and placed my hands on his chest. His heart thumped furiously. I relaxed in his embrace and buried my face in the warm space between his neck and shoulder, breathing him in slowly.

"It's been a long day, Serena. Just sleep," he whispered into my hair.

His body heat seeped into mine, and I closed my eyes. I waited to fall asleep while replaying more of the memories he'd shown me during our mind-meld. I watched through his eyes as he saw me for the very first time, back at the fae palace. He'd said that I had just happened to tag along during the spell by accident; that he'd only aimed to get my brother, Vita, and Aida back to Eritopia.

But I could see myself in the palace, laughing with the girls, surrounded by gorgeous fae during the dinner. I felt what he'd felt in that moment—a strange heat pouring through his veins as he stared at me through his flame. He'd been watching for a while before we were zapped into his mansion in Eritopia.

With all the craziness that happened after we kissed, I didn't even get to talk to Draven about this particular memory. As his memories warped into shapes and colors dripping around me like a psychedelic rain, I slipped into a dream.

SERENA

I must've slept for a long time. It felt like forever. I peeled my eyes open and noticed the sun still peeking shyly from the east through the window. I realized I'd completely blacked out for almost twenty hours.

Wow.

I breathed in deeply, eerily accustomed to the faint smell of dampness that lingered throughout the house, and quickly went over the previous day's events in my mind. I started with Draven pulling me into his arms before we fell asleep and moved backward through each key moment.

My guilt still ate away at me for breaking the Daughter's shell in my desperately foolish attempt to release and retrieve my brother.

I huffed with frustration and rubbed my eyes with the back of my hands. My mind raced back to the dead succubi scouts slumped over their horses, silver blood pouring out of their fatal wounds.

My fingers ran over the soft blanket, and I realized I was alone in bed.

I thought of Draven, our kiss, and the unbelievably profound mind-meld. I had never been so close to anyone in my life.

I could still hear his heartbeat drumming in my ears. I could feel his chest burning every time he looked at me.

I seemed to have an effect on him strangely similar to the effect he had on me, but the way he experienced feelings was much more intense, as if he was hypersensitive by nature.

I made a mental note to look for some encyclopedia on Druids downstairs and read up on his species. I still had questions about his memories, but this would have to wait until we were calm and alone again. We had a long day ahead of us before that.

Where is he?

His absence made me groan. I sat up and nearly jumped out of bed at the sight of him quietly sitting in the armchair.

"Sheesh. You startled me!" I snapped, running a hand through my hair as I recovered my breath.

He was fully dressed, with his legs crossed. Tousled hair framed his face.

"I was waiting for you to wake up," he said.

"Ah, well, I'm up," I replied with an ounce of sarcasm and got out of bed.

I stretched my arms out and reveled in the sound of my spine crackling, relieving days' worth of pressure and stress.

"Let me just wash my face," I said and dashed into the bathroom.

I welcomed the cold water splashing against my face and neck, but I still felt weak and hungry—the kind of hunger that I could only soothe by syphoning. It hit me then that I hadn't fed since we first got to the mansion. No wonder I was so mellow. I hoped that Jovi or Field were at full operating capacity that morning. I needed some nourishment, and they were the strongest ones in our pack.

The Druid's energy oozed off him deliciously. I immediately sensed it once I got out of the bathroom. I'd been successful at tuning it out, but I was hungry. I craved his energy the most, but I wasn't sure whether he'd want me to feed off him.

Draven stood up, and I moved in front of him, close enough to take his hand and place it on my shoulder for guidance. I opened the bedroom door and took a step toward the corridor. His touch sent flickers of electricity through my limbs.

His fingers tightened their grip on me and pulled me back, turning me around in the process. I didn't have any time to react to his move. I stilled as his lips came down on mine in a gentle kiss.

It was completely unexpected. My raw instincts simmered to the surface, and I opened my mouth to take everything he had to offer. Fire burned in my stomach as he deepened the kiss, our tongues caressing each other.

He wrapped his arms around me, drawing me into his marble-like body, and I softened against him. Pressure built up between us, setting off a rain of sparks. Our kiss reached a new peak of intensity as we devoured each other.

His fingers vanished beneath my shirt, cool against my skin and sending shivers down my spine. I gasped in response and snaked my arms around his neck. His thumbs moved lightly over my ribs, dangerously close to my breasts.

He let out a raspy moan and took me even deeper into the kiss, pushing me against the door frame and using the weight of his body to hold me there. I ran one hand through his hair, while the other hooked around his neck for support. My legs had given up. My core trembled, and my heart pumped incandescent blood through my veins.

I was so hungry for him, I felt my primal side clawing at the inside of my skin begging to claim and consume him. I pushed back into his kiss, biting into his lower lip to send him a message— I wanted him as badly as he wanted me, and I could no longer fight that. He grunted and stilled. His lips parted, and his hot breath fluttered over my face. He captured my mouth again, his fingers digging into my hips, my flesh tender under his touch.

Heat spread through the lower half of my body, and his thigh pushed its way between my legs, further anchoring me to the door frame. I held on for dear life. My mind was devoid of everything but him. I felt his heady, vibrant energy glaze over me, warming my skin like sunshine.

It was right there within my reach, and I nearly gave in and allowed myself to syphon off him without bothering to ask for permission. He was so hot and delicious and consuming like a wild forest fire. Any closer, and I would burn up like a moth in the flame.

The sound of footsteps coming downstairs crashed through our heady bubble. Jovi and Field spoke as they went into the banquet room, and the double doors thudded behind them.

Everything stopped.

Draven pulled away, leaving my lips swollen, raw, and wanting more.

His hand pushed against the doorframe just above my head, as he leaned into it for support. He panted, slowly recovering his breath. I was even worse, gasping for air and unsteady on my feet. My whole body trembled, so close, yet too far from his.

We spent several minutes like that, quietly breathing in and out in a peculiar unison as we struggled to regain some kind of composure. I needed to focus on something other than his lips, glistening red from our kiss.

Coffee. I need coffee. Focus on coffee.

I cleared my throat and straightened my back, then took his hand in mine. His palm was warm, and his fingertips brushed against mine, tickling my senses.

"Okay, let's um…let's get some breakfast," I managed to say.

A smile lifted the corners of his mouth as he nodded.

I would have dragged him back into the bedroom in that

moment, to do more of what we'd just stopped doing, to find refuge in his arms, and to satisfy the yearning he'd nurtured in my heart, but reality came back with an unpleasant thud. We had work to do.

We reached the banquet hall, and I placed his hand on my shoulder. I didn't want everyone to see us holding hands. It would have prompted the girls to question me—not that I had a problem with that, but I would have to explain something that I didn't fully understand myself.

I knew how it felt, but I didn't yet know how to put it into words.

Vita

As we all gathered in the dining hall for breakfast, I noticed the predominance of puffy eyes in our group. We'd all slept heavily after the previous morning's ordeal, and I welcomed the feeling of absolute rest—I had no other name for so many consecutive hours spent sleeping. I could see everything in a different light, more clearly and optimistically than before.

Come to think of it, despite the impending doom of Azazel and the threat he posed on our lives, I was strangely content. We were all there, friends and strangers gathered around the table, eating the same breakfast as yesterday and the days before that, gulping down coffee and remembering The Shade and how easy life had been prior to Eritopia. A tinge of melancholy lingered between us, hung between memories of our parents and our play fights after GASP training sessions.

Even so, none of us seemed as lost or as hopeless as our first days in the mansion; our experience here had brought us closer together, as friends and family. We'd even made new friends who were about as weird as we were.

I watched quietly as Aida and Jovi poked fun at each other over their physical training sessions back home, and Serena talked to Bijarki, Anjani, and Draven about the next steps in our mission to defeat Azazel. At the other end of the table, Phoenix ate quietly with the Daughter sitting next to him. She watched him take generous bites out of his pancakes.

"If the Dearghs join our alliance, we'll have an impressive advantage in the battlefield," Draven said to Serena.

"What *are* the Dearghs, anyway? I've heard you talking about them, but I have no idea what they are." Serena stuck a piece of bread in her mouth and chewed.

"The Dearghs are guardians of Eritopia's volcanoes, servants of nature," Anjani explained.

At the sound of her voice, Jovi forgot all about his quips with Aida and turned his head to listen to the succubus.

Soon enough, Aida and Field also focused their attention on Anjani. Given the awkwardness between them, and the stolen glances, I had a feeling that Aida was looking for something to focus on other than Field. She'd spent her life admiring him from afar and keeping her distance, but since his breakup with Maura,

Field had slowly shifted toward Aida.

"They're stone giants," Anjani continued, picking at a pancake with her fingers. "They're born from the volcanoes, and they spend their whole lives around them. They live for thousands of years, and their lifelines are tied to the volcano that brought them into the world. If the volcano dies out, so do the Dearghs it birthed."

"How many volcanoes are there on this planet?" asked Jovi, his eyes locked on the succubus.

"There used to be dozens, and each represented a clan of Dearghs. Now, since Azazel has been tearing this world apart, there are only ten active volcanoes left. Ten clans," she replied.

"What does Azazel have to do with the volcanoes, though?" Serena asked.

"Azazel uses powerful dark magic to conquer Eritopia. This magic draws its energy from nature, and it's all-consuming when used on a grand scale," Draven explained. "It takes tremendous amounts of power for him to corrupt his Destroyers, not to mention the war campaigns against the incubi citadels and all his other dirty tricks. Volcanoes are a great source of such power, and Azazel has been abusing them for decades now, draining them out with no regard for what that does to the Dearghs."

"If anything, Azazel would be much happier if he could wipe out all the Dearghs, like he did with the storm hounds," Bijarki interjected. A frown settled between his straight eyebrows. "They're deadly in battle, although it takes forever to get a Deargh angry enough to fight."

The Dearghs sounded a lot like my fae kind—lovers of the natural elements. They were apparently gentle and peaceful despite their massive size and fire powers.

It hit me then that, with all the madness of yesterday, I hadn't told the girls or anyone else about my newly awakened fire fae abilities. I spent a few minutes thinking about how I would break the news to them. I didn't want to tell them and then watch a flame fizzle out in absolute failure in case I didn't focus enough, so instead I decided to surprise them.

I stood up slowly and picked one of the candles resting at the center of the dining table—a long white wax stick set in a beautiful silver holder with brushed ornate details swirling down to the base.

I looked around. Everyone was engaged in conversations about the Dearghs and the Destroyers and who would win in a fight between the two. Bijarki was the only one watching me.

I took a matchbox and lit the candle, then breathed deeply and followed the steps I'd taken during my previous fae session under the magnolia tree. I emptied my head of everything, shutting out the noises and focusing on Bijarki. He seemed to do the trick for me then, so it was worth trying again. I channeled my attention on him, drawing him into my mind, and placed my palms above the small flame.

It flickered for a while, and I pulled my hands outward, slowly, as if using them to expand the fire. I coaxed my innermost self to connect with it and urged it to grow. Much to my delight, the flame grew into an incandescent fire sphere the size of a soccer ball,

72

sizzling and crackling under my control. I felt my lips turn into a smile. I worked the flame until it grew big enough to stop everyone from talking. It demanded attention with its size and awe-inspiring burn.

I kept my energy focused on the spherical blaze, but my eyes wandered around the table. They were all stunned, eyes wide and mouths gaping, except for Draven, who only stilled and listened carefully.

Serena and Aida were the first to stand up, gasping and clapping their hands as if watching the greatest circus trick ever. By all definitions, it was exactly that—a wonderful little trick—but I had spent so much time trying to make it happen that their sheer joy nurtured my soul. I expanded the flame further as I fed off their positive energy. Everyone else pushed themselves out of their chairs and took a couple of steps back to avoid the heat.

I was impressed by how big I had made it. I let out a long, unwinding sigh and willed the flame into submission. It dimmed slowly and unraveled in a fiery spiral, following the circular motions of my fingers, swirling around like an incandescent ribbon.

Serena burst into laughter and clapped again, and I noticed Jovi, Phoenix, and Field grinning with delight as they watched me literally playing with fire. Bijarki wore a different smile; fascination flickered in his silver-blue eyes. Anjani had her head cocked to one side, eyes squinting slightly and the corners of her mouth turned upward. The Daughter stared with childish astonishment, reminding me of Serena's expression when we were only five, and Grandpa Ben showed us one of his fae fireworks across the water on Halloween night.

"Oh, my God, Vita!" Serena exclaimed, finally finding her words.

"You did it! You freaking did it!" Aida chimed in.

My heart burst at the sight of my friends' unadulterated joy about my achievement. I had been so fortunate to have them in my life. They had encouraged me along the way to never give up, to always keep trying until I did it. So I'd finally done it, and a sense of pride filled me up. I was finally able to show them that all their kind words had led to something great.

I nodded with a sheepish smile and put the flame out, feeling the tips of my fingers buzzing with heat. With a little more practice—well, actually a lot more practice—I would be able to turn these fiery tricks into actual weapons. I was only part-fae, but I still had potential. I'd been raised to believe that hard work added on top of natural talent could make extraordinary things happen, and my little candle trick was the shy beginning of one such endeavor. I could feel it in my gut.

"I totally did." I grinned.

Anjani described to Draven what I had just done, and I saw a smile pass over his face. I looked around again and saw Bijarki's gaze soften, a smile blooming on his face too.

"So, from now on we need to be careful with the fae jokes, otherwise you'll set us on fire, huh?" Jovi grinned, wrapping his arm around my shoulder and pulling me closer.

"Yeah, she's a fiery sprite all right," Phoenix quipped.

"Mind your tongue, sentry," I replied primly, pointing a finger at his chest.

Everyone chuckled, and I felt truly happy, despite our circumstances. We had a long day ahead of us, but we needed this little bit of fun to relieve the tension and shed some light on the gloom that had recently seeped into our souls.

"I'm impressed," Bijarki said huskily.

Our eyes met, and I nodded. My cheeks burned. His acknowledgment of my fae abilities had quite an impact on my senses.

"It took me a long time to get to this," I explained. "It turns out, all I have to do is open up to everything that I feel and harness the power that my emotions generate. The fae live life to the fullest, fusing with the elements in the process. I just had to understand this process on my own terms."

"By allowing yourself to feel everything, even that which you had previously denied yourself," the incubus said.

I blushed as I caught the undertone of his statement. I figured he was testing me, trying to hone in on my feelings, to ascertain whether I felt something for him.

My knees weakened as I remembered his earlier confession. I didn't know where to begin with telling him about how I felt. I'd do better fighting a Destroyer right then and there than telling Bijarki that I was attracted to him.

"I'm sorry I can't see your fae abilities for myself," said Draven. "I've only read about your kind, and I could never get close enough to see one of you in action."

Serena looked at him, a pained expression in her eyes. There was definitely something there between them, something that I hadn't seen before. Her irises shone every time her gaze found him, as if he was the most important creature in the room. We'd have to talk about that later. We'd been so busy surviving in Eritopia that we'd barely had a moment to ourselves as friends to simply talk and knock heads on the more trivial things.

"Nevertheless, if you harness this ability to its full potential, you will be extremely useful in the days ahead, especially when we go against the Destroyers," Draven continued.

"You think?" I asked, trying to imagine the steps I'd need to take in order to reach that level of power.

"Absolutely. Nothing is more effective in a war than fire and disease. You hold the power of fire in your fingertips."

The gravity of that statement weighed heavily on me. It involved killing other creatures, and it was something that I wasn't sure I was capable of. Death was so final. I couldn't wrap my head around the concept.

"I'll have to keep practicing." I changed the subject. "Grandpa Ben often said that if I can command one element, I can command all of them, and now I'm curious."

Serena laughed as we all resumed our seats at the table, halfway through breakfast.

"One day at a time, champ!" She refilled her coffee cup. "You've made it this far. I have no doubt you'll have the rest down in no time."

I smiled at her, wondering if she was right.

PHOENIX

We all settled back into our seats after Vita's display.

I was genuinely thrilled to see Vita coming into her own with her fae abilities. As tiny and as introverted as she usually was, she had taken on a new form in Eritopia. Someone once said that the prettiest flower bloomed in adversity. The dire circumstances seemed to have channeled the greatness within her to meet the potential that she probably wasn't sure she had. Her happiness was our happiness.

I ate another pancake and washed it down with coffee. The Daughter sat next to me, quiet and curious, watching my every move with childlike interest. The way I chewed, the way I drank, the way I laughed and smiled—they were all of interest to her, as if she was watching a movie. Judging by the glimmer in her violet eyes, it was a movie she liked.

She hadn't eaten anything, so I wondered whether a Daughter of Eritopia needed nourishment or not and how I could help. I looked at her once in a while, giving her a candid smile as I worked through my breakfast.

However, I couldn't just let her sit there, so I placed one of my oaty pancakes on her plate and drizzled what I had decided to call maybe-maple-syrup over it. She looked at it curiously, cocking her head with a frown.

"You should eat. It's actually quite good," I encouraged her.

"What is this?"

"Not sure what they call it here, but back home we call it a pancake. Also, I'm not sure whether you eat, or what you should eat, but I think this is a good place to start." I smiled and handed her a fork.

She looked at it, a foreign silver object to her, and set it on the table. Clearly, she didn't see the point of it. Instead, she picked the pancake up with two fingers and took a small bite out of it. A drop of syrup slipped down her lower lip. My stomach tightened at the sight, and I instinctively licked my lower lip in response.

She chewed a couple of times before she swallowed and crinkled her nose.

"I'm sorry there's not much on the menu here." I sighed and looked at Draven, who was engaged in conversation with Serena.

"I don't like it," the Daughter replied, then dropped the

pancake back on the plate.

"The house is protected by ancient magic. The Druid calls them wards. They're the ones who replenish our food and supplies every day, but they're not too creative in the cooking department, I'm afraid," I explained.

The Daughter looked around the banquet hall, as if searching for something.

"I mean, I'd give anything for some fresh fruits, for example, but I've pretty much gotten used to this stuff. We need the nourishment, so we'll take what we can get." I watched her eyes dart around the room.

Her gaze settled on something.

I looked in that direction but saw nothing other than a light breeze moving one of the off-white curtains by the window.

"This is powerful magic though, put in place by your sisters, the Daughters of Eritopia," I continued, hoping to maybe trigger some memory or knowledge in her mind.

I figured that maybe if I talked about the Daughters and this world, she might eventually remember what she needed to remember. I wasn't sure whether the other Daughters had been born with any knowledge of their existence or not. Based on what the Druid had told us, they'd always been around, for as long as there was a recorded history of Eritopia, but no one knew who created them.

"My sisters," the Daughter said absently, her eyes following something around the table.

"Do you see something?" I asked, unable to understand what she was looking at so intently.

"You said there are ancient wards here."

"Yes," I replied slowly.

"I think I see them."

My mind came to a halt. Judging by the looks on everyone's faces, they were as surprised as I was to hear the Daughter say that. We never saw anything around the house that wasn't old and dusty and worn out by the passage of time. No magical creature, just wood, tattered fabrics, and decay.

"What do you mean you can see them?" I asked.

"The wards," she looked at me, then pointed at one of the windows. "There's one there, waiting for us to finish eating, I think."

She then pointed at a cabinet at the door that led to the kitchen and an empty space next to Draven. I couldn't see anything, not even when I tried my True Sight. My mental energy was low. I needed to syphon from someone soon. But still, nothing.

"They're here. I can see them," the Daughter said absently.

"You can see the wards." Draven repeated her statement from across the table, as if he couldn't believe it either.

"Yes. Phoenix said they were made by my sisters, and when he said that, I thought about it, and I could suddenly see them."

A moment passed as we all tried to digest that precious little snippet of information. As soon as she'd been told about her sister's magic, she was able to see it. The wheels in my mind started turning with potential scenarios, and I decided to speak to the Druid about it later. Perhaps we could unlock more of her powers if we told her more about her sisters and what purpose they served in Eritopia.

"What do they look like?" Draven asked.

"They don't have a particular shape. They're like…they're like liquid shadows, floating around. They don't have faces or limbs, but they change their forms, from what I can tell. They're strange." The Daughter described them with a tinge of amusement in her voice.

"How can she see them suddenly?" Serena asked no one in particular, looking around the hall as if trying to find the wards herself.

"It might have something to do with awareness," Draven said. "Maybe if she's told about something of hers, or something related to her being or her abilities, then she becomes aware of it and can see it."

The Daughter stood up and started looking beneath the warming dishes laid out on the table, lifting one cover at a time. She found a pot filled with what looked like porridge, steaming hot.

"Yeah, we don't usually touch that," Aida said. "It doesn't look that great and it smells even worse."

The Daughter then put the cover back, closed her eyes, and took a deep breath. A smile tugged at the corners of her mouth. She looked around, as if following the wards in their silent motion and removed the cover from the porridge pot once more.

Vita gasped, as she was the closest to it. Her turquoise eyes widened at the sight of the contents. I had to stand up to get a better look, and my jaw dropped. The porridge was gone completely. It had been replaced by a multitude of fruits of all shapes and sizes, glistening in exotic shades of red, green, and purple.

"What are those?" Aida asked, fascinated by this new development.

She picked up one of the fruits that resembled a red plum and sniffed it. Her smile told me it smelled good. It probably tasted even better.

I picked one up and took a bite. My teeth sank into the tender flesh, and a smooth, bittersweet flavor invaded my mouth. It was delicious and sweet but with a bit of a punch.

"This is good. How'd you do this?" I asked the Daughter.

She looked up and gave me a shy smile. Her hands fiddled with a lock of reddish pink hair.

"You said you wanted fruits so…I asked the wards to give you fruits."

Her response was simple, yet mind-boggling. I was officially impressed. Moreover, I was delighted by the taste, so I tried another one—a small purple berry. I crushed it between my teeth, and it immediately reminded me of the blackberries from the woods back home.

Finally, something other than those bland pancakes!

"You commanded the wards to change the food?" Draven asked, after Serena told him what had happened.

"I could hear them in my mind, whispering and shuffling about, talking about their chores for the day." The Daughter nodded. "So, I reached out to them and asked them for fruits. They listened."

"This is unbelievable," Serena tried one that reminded me of wild green apples. "They taste so good!"

Soon enough, we had forgotten all about the regular menu and were stuffing our faces with fruits, exhilarated by the plethora of sweetness and freshness.

The Daughter sat down and ate some herself, beaming with satisfaction and watching me as I conquered another plum. I smiled back, thankful to have her around. Something told me there were more surprises coming from her soon enough. I just had to make sure that she would stay on our side once she attained the knowledge required to wield her clearly godlike powers.

"You connected with the wards somehow," Draven mused.

The Daughter looked at him.

"The magic was crafted by your sisters, so it must have resonated with you. Not even my father could do what you just did," he continued. "There's definitely power in you, although latent. I just don't know what it will take or how long it will take to harness it all. Or what you can do, for that matter."

She nodded slowly and looked down, as if suddenly unhappy with her current condition. I couldn't really blame her—not knowing who or what you were but being able to influence ancient magic wards must be intense and confusing.

I reached under the table, took her hand in mine, and squeezed it gently. My stomach churned every time I saw glimpses of sadness flickering across her beautiful face. This creature wasn't meant to feel miserable or maladjusted. I wanted her glowing and happy.

Our eyes met, and I felt my whole body heat up. My heartbeat accelerated, and I gave her another smile. She returned it with grace as our fingers intertwined. Her touch was incredibly soft, fluttering over my skin like a summer breeze.

I had a lot to understand about her, but everything about her felt like ecstasy wrapped up in a dark mystery. It was either going to kill me or make me the happiest creature in all the worlds.

AIDA

The day was off to a surprisingly positive start. It made me feel like, despite the disastrous previous couple of days and Azazel's advance on the incubi nation, we still might be able to pull through this after all.

None of us knew how, but having this glimmer of hope gave us enough strength to stand up from that breakfast table and head downstairs into the basement for another Tap-the-Oracle session.

To say I wasn't particularly excited about it would be an understatement. The visions so far hadn't shown me anything positive—just doubt and cruelty—but I had to go deeper into my abilities as an Oracle. Vita's progress on her fire fae power had given me a little competitive push; she was already quite far down the road with her visions, as opposed to Phoenix and me. After all, she'd had them outside the controlled sessions with the Druid, whereas I still struggled with the aftermath of my last incursion.

The memory of black runes dancing across my skin that night still sent shivers down my spine. I reached the basement room with its hospital beds and medicine cabinets. Bijarki fired up the oil lamps, and Anjani prepared a special mixture of herbs for us.

As if knowing the drill already, Vita, Phoenix, and I each took one bed, lying on our backs and waiting for the Druid's instructions. Anjani filled a wooden bowl with several plants, including the petals of a peculiar type of scarlet rose with contrasting white edges.

I leaned on my elbows and watched as she blended everything with smooth, circular wrist movements, using a wide silver spoon. Draven sat on a stool with Serena standing next to him, watching over us with a concerned expression. Knowing her, she worried about us more than we worried about ourselves. I caught her gaze and threw her a crooked smile and a wink to show her that everything was going to be okay.

I had no way of knowing that for sure, but she didn't need to know that.

"What's that you're making?" I asked Anjani, trying to keep my mind focused on something other than the searing presence of Field next to my bed. I could feel his breath gently brushing against my hair from above.

"It's a proprietary blend we make in our tribe to really expand our senses," the succubus replied as she continued mixing the herbs together. "During the full moon, the succubi ingest this and transcend everything, as our innermost senses commune with nature. It's hard to explain what it actually does, but the Druid tells me you need to disconnect yourselves from this world in order to tap into your Oracle visions. This mixture will help."

"What's in it?" Vita asked.

I looked over to get a quick look at my little fire fae friend.

Bijarki stood by her bedside, quiet and thoughtful. His gaze never left her face except to occasionally wander along the entire length of her body. Judging by the glimmer in his eyes, he found her attractive even in those brown velvet slacks and the ivory shirt she'd settled on—both items normally worn by men about two hundred years ago.

"Most of the plants I gathered from the Druid's greenhouse, some roots and stems of arrowhead, Moraine shrubs, and demon tears," Anjani explained.

I didn't know what any of those plants were, but I nodded nonetheless.

"I brought spiced rose petals from the camp, though. You can't find those just anywhere."

"What's a spiced rose?" I asked.

"It's a rare flower that grows on the outskirts of tall limestone mountains such as the one where our tribe lives. It's the main ingredient for this mixture, as it opens up one's senses. You hear more, you see more, and you feel and taste things you'd otherwise never notice. It enhances everything, while the other herbs serve as additional amplifiers, accelerating the spiced rose's effects throughout the body."

As she explained what the flower did, I couldn't help but notice the fleeting glances between Anjani and Jovi. I could've sworn I saw my brother blush, and I had a feeling that there was a story behind that spiced rose that I didn't know. Yet. I was going to have a little chat with my brother after all this was over.

"I've had some unpleasant experiences with herb mixtures meant to hone in on my Oracle abilities," Phoenix interjected.

Jovi moved to stand by his bedside and watch over him, but the Daughter politely pushed him away, asserting her status as Phoenix's caregiver.

"I will take care of him," she said, her voice sharper than usual.

If she weren't a potentially deadly goddess, I would've said she was downright adorable.

My brother smiled sheepishly and moved back next to Serena. His gaze darted around the room but eventually settled on Anjani.

There is definitely something between them.

"You mean you almost died," Serena said to her brother.

"Not my fault!"

"Technically, it was my fault," Draven interrupted.

"It won't happen with this," Anjani assured him, taking the bowl in her hand and coming to Phoenix's bedside. "The dose is minimal, and based on what the Druid told me about your abilities, it will not overcharge you. You need to suck on this for a minute, then swallow it."

She loaded the spoon with the heady mixture and fed it to Phoenix. He chewed on the blend, slowly getting accustomed to the taste. He lifted an eyebrow and looked at me, then Vita.

"This doesn't taste bad, actually."

Anjani then moved over to my bed and gave me some as well. I chewed and sucked on the pulpy mixture for a while. I was surprised by its rich flavors. They reminded me of a stew made with an abundance of cinnamon and pepper. I then swallowed it and let my head drop back on the pillow. I looked up and found Field's turquoise eyes scanning me carefully, while Anjani fed the rest of the mixture to Vita.

"Now we wait for the spiced rose to spread out and untangle your senses," Draven said. "You'll most likely feel a slight tingling, then everything will open up to you. That's when you'll be able to fully relax into it and focus on the past, the present, and the future. Based on our own experiences with the flower, I figured it was a good bet to try for your Oracle abilities."

I listened to the Druid's voice as I felt the world around me vibrate. Field's fingers brushed gently against my shoulders, and I felt his touch deep inside me, as if he'd reached into my very soul. I smiled, and I heard his heart thudding in his chest, the air whistling in and out of his lungs, the blood rushing through his veins.

My limbs tingled, and I felt a velvety warmth glazing me from head to toe. I relaxed into it, taking deep breaths as my eyelids began to feel heavy. My head slowly dropped to the side, and I could see Phoenix in his bed, the Daughter standing next to him.

His eyes closed, and I figured he was the first to go under. I took another breath and felt my body melt and expand outward, transcending time, space, and matter.

I saw the Daughter as she rolled her eyes and passed out, collapsing on the floor with a loud thud. It prompted Anjani and Jovi to rush over to her.

Everything warped, and darkness enveloped me.

SERENA

It happened so fast. One moment I was watching my brother close his eyes as the spiced rose mixture took over, and the next I saw the Daughter drop to the floor. Jovi and Anjani reached her in seconds, lifting her onto a spare bed.

"What's wrong with her?" I asked, my breath short.

"What happened?" Draven asked.

"The Daughter collapsed," I said to him.

Anjani looked for vitals.

Yesterday Anjani couldn't feel her heartbeat, so I wondered how she'd be able to tell whether the Daughter was alive or not. My blood froze at the thought of her dying while in our care. Her sisters would probably wipe us off the face of the planet with a snap of their fingers. No—they would make us suffer first.

Anjani lowered her head, her ear close enough to the Daughter's lips to register breathing. "She's alive," the succubus said.

Relief washed over me. I sighed and instinctively leaned against Draven for support.

"She must have passed out," Anjani continued, her fingers looking for a pulse. "Her breathing is even, and I can see movement beneath her eyelids."

"That's curious," Draven mumbled. "Passing out at the same time as Phoenix."

"Do you think there's a connection between their consciousnesses?" I asked, trying to think of reasons why that would happen.

"I'm not sure," he replied. "Anjani, can you please keep watch over her, just in case?"

The succubus nodded and kept her stance by the Daughter's bedside.

Jovi moved over to watch Phoenix during his immersion. I looked over to my brother, then Aida and Vita. They were deep under, their chests rising and falling slowly and evenly.

We'd reached a point in the dynamic of things where we could no longer rely on Draven for information about the Daughter. Given her condition, courtesy of my blunder, we couldn't tell what would have been deemed as normal and what was weird in this entire situation. All we could do was keep an eye out and try to paddle our way through the unknown.

I couldn't help but wonder where the Daughters were. They must have sensed that their sister was awake. I'd ask Draven about that later. He might know something.

In the meantime, however, I shifted my focus back to my brother and friends.

Aida

I stood in absolute darkness with no sound or sense of anything.

"Hello?" I called out, hoping that this wasn't going to be my vision.

It was tough enough that I had to see what was happening in real time without being able to stop or change any of it. Being stuck in the darkness throughout an entire vision would've added a whole new level of uselessness to my gift.

The blackness dissipated, and I found myself in the middle of what looked like a jungle with massively tall trees as thick as buildings and reaching so high it looked like they must brush the sky. Giant green and yellow leaves with waxy surfaces emerged from the foliage. Beautiful pink and white exotic flowers blossomed on the ground supported by a bed of tall grass and black ferns.

I could hear birds singing from the tree crowns and what sounded like insects whistling and crackling below. Before I could move, three creatures passed right through me, as if I were made of smoke.

"Do you think they'll work with us, Chief?" one asked the other.

They followed the trail that unraveled ahead of me, snaking through the forest toward what looked like an enormous mountain with black ridges and dense purple forests. It looked beautifully weird as it towered above us.

I looked at the creatures ahead—feminine figures with long black hair cascading down their backs, familiar-looking silvery skin, and husky voices. Their voluptuous curves were clad in thick black leathers, and stripes of red paint crossed their bodies in a diagonal pattern down their arms and legs. They carried heavy swords in metallic scabbards with bone sculpture details on the handles. Crossbows and quivers with short arrows hung on their backs, and bright red feathers were braided through their hair.

They had to be succubi.

I decided to follow them as they walked toward the black mountain.

The sound of thunder boomed from above, but as I looked up, the sky was perfectly clear and blue. The rumble continued somewhere in the distance, and the ground trembled beneath us.

"The volcano is fired up," said one of the succubi.

"It must be giving birth to a new Deargh," the one in the middle mused.

"Is that possible in this day and age?"

"It might be. I wouldn't put anything past Eritopia. As for your question, Lessa, they have every reason to form an alliance with us and the Druid against this bastard, Azazel," replied the succubus in the middle.

A red cape hung loosely from her shoulder, prompting me to think that perhaps she was the leader of the party. She seemed slightly taller and bigger than the other two. In my head, it was anthropology 101—the person with the most decoration and muscles was most likely the chief.

We reached a clearing, where I was momentarily distracted by an explosion of flowers in pinks, purples, and fiery reds. The dizzying array of flowers all around us was bordered by giant trees. Right across this clearing was a cluster of giant limestone rocks, apparently rooted to the ground.

They seemed to have been carved into relatively human shapes with arms, legs, and square faces. Green vines had climbed all over them, spreading out and blossoming with small white flowers.

The succubi stopped in front of these stone giants. There were four of them, I realized as we got closer.

"Good day, kind Dearghs," the succubus in the middle shouted at the rocks. "We've come to speak to Urdi, your chief."

For a moment, I thought she might've lost her marbles in the jungle since she was talking to a rock, but when said rock started crackling and moving, I stilled, my mouth gaping. The stone giants were very much alive. They straightened their massive limestone backs slowly—they'd probably been in those positions for a long time. After all, they had vines growing all over them. This whole tableau brought back memories of old Viking folk tales I'd read as a kid about Norwegian stone giants.

"Good day to you, Hansa of the Red Tribe," one of the Dearghs responded, his voice solid, like rocks crashing against each other. He took a step forward and bowed, each movement seeming like an extraordinary effort for the limestone titan.

Hansa, the one I'd identified as the leader, bowed in response. I took a few steps forward, standing between the succubi and the Dearghs and watched the exchange like a game of tennis.

"Thank you for speaking to us," Hansa replied. "We bring news from the north of an alliance between our tribe and a Druid against Azazel's reign of terror."

"What makes you think we are interested in war, succubus? We are creatures of peace."

"While that is true, I believe Urdi will want to hear what we have to say." Hansa smirked with self-confidence. "Especially once he hears the reason behind your volcanoes dying out. This war involves all of Eritopia, whether you like it or not."

The Deargh thought about it for a few seconds, then nodded and stepped aside. The other stone giants did the same, clearing the path ahead for the succubi. I walked with them as they advanced through the clearing, passed the Dearghs, and entered another space. This one was blanketed by tall grass for a few dozen yards before it rose into a stony ridge leading to a plateau above.

We climbed the mountain via this ridge, and I couldn't help but admire the view as we went. The jungle unraveled at our feet in shades of deep green and yellow. The tall trees brushed against white wisps of clouds. It was breathtaking—a lavish wilderness that was a natural masterpiece. Strings of birds flew across as the sun threw colorful reflections from their pink, red, and turquoise feathers.

I turned around and saw a massive limestone wall rising above me. It continued upward into another, sharper ridge. From the wall emerged about a dozen Dearghs, as if passing through a waterfall. They stood so tall that I had to crane my neck in order to see their faces. They reminded me a little of the Easter Island statues, their features rough and simple.

One Deargh stood out in particular with black stone inserts throughout his body like obsidian tattoos. He was bigger than the others, and his eyes were deep set below the shadow of the horizontal ridge, glimmering orange like two small fires.

"Urdi," Hansa addressed him directly. "It's been too long!"

She smiled and bowed respectfully, and the other two succubi followed her lead. Urdi, the chief of these Dearghs, from what I assumed, nodded in return. His breath was heavy, as if every movement was a daunting task.

"Hansa, sister of the Red Tribe," he replied. "What brings you here after five hundred years?"

"Eritopia is in danger, milord, and you know very well why," the succubus said in a grave tone. "Azazel is spewing darkness and poison all over the world, and many are dying. You know that we can't have that. It's not natural."

"We are well aware of Azazel and his Destroyers. But it does not concern us, my dear. We are bound to our volcanoes and speak to no one. For as long as Eritopia stands, we stand. That is not something he can change, regardless of his power."

"But that is where you're wrong, milord. We are all creatures of Eritopia, and we all deserve to live. Just because you think his reign doesn't affect you, that doesn't mean you should just stand back and watch everything burn," Hansa replied. "People are dying. The planet is drenched in blood."

She took a step forward, tilted her head to one side, and crossed her arms. The other Dearghs closed in on us, tightening the circle. Their shadows fell heavily on us, but Hansa did not budge.

"Besides, you don't seem to realize how much damage Azazel has done to your kind already," she continued.

Urdi straightened his back in response.

"What do you mean?" he asked.

"Why do you think the volcanoes have been dying over the past few centuries, Urdi?"

"It is nature's will. Eritopia gives life but it also takes life. We have made our peace with that."

"So you're perfectly fine with hundreds of Dearghs perishing when volcanoes die out one after the other, while Azazel's power grows stronger every day?" Hansa replied.

"What does one have to do with the other?"

The succubus threw her head back and laughed, mockery underlining her tone. Judging by the dark, stern looks on the Dearghs' faces, I hoped she would soon deliver the answer to Urdi's question before the succubi were all crushed beneath giant limestone fists.

"Wow, Urdi. You've been around for thousands of years, and yet you fail to see how Azazel's power grew while your brothers started dying out! I'm disappointed," she said. "Open your eyes, Dearghs!"

Her voice shot through the silence and echoed across the plateau.

"Azazel draws power from the volcanoes for his dark magic. The energy from these active mountains doesn't just keep you Dearghs alive. It feeds his ability to corrupt and consume. It's how he's created Destroyers from Druids! It's how he's led successful campaigns against the incubi citadels. He rained fire and brimstone upon them! It's how he keeps his spying eyes and ears open throughout Eritopia! Your life for his dark magic!"

The Dearghs stilled and blinked several times, their stone eyelids scratching against each other.

"Azazel is draining our volcanoes?" came Urdi's reply, laced with disbelief.

"Yes! We know that for a fact, as we, too, have some eyes inside his city. It's why he's gained so much power in the first place, why so many incubi would rather bow before him than fight him."

For a taut moment, Urdi stared silently at Hansa, taking in her words.

Then Urdi dropped to one knee before Hansa. "I will summon our brothers from the other clans today, succubus. Stay here, and join our council tonight," he said.

"Your volcanoes are spread across the planet, Urdi. How will they all be here by tonight?" Hansa lifted an eyebrow.

"The volcano fires are portals from one mountain to another, my dear. It's how we travel."

I wanted to hear more, but before I could catch the rest of the exchange between Hansa and Urdi, the image before me dissolved into absolute darkness. I groaned.

* * *

Next thing I knew, I found myself standing in a narrow corridor with small green fires burning overhead in bronze plates hung from the ceiling. The flames threw peculiar lights across the black stone walls.

Several archways were carved ahead, leading to different chambers. As I walked forward, my ears captured noises from behind—shrills of pain and broken pleas. I didn't like this place at all. Paralyzing terror threatened to wrap around my limbs.

I took a deep breath, reminding myself that this was just a vision and that I could not be harmed. I noticed a yellow light flickering ahead, where the corridor ended in another chamber. I passed through it and walked into a spacious room with a tall ceiling and torches mounted on the walls.

The floor glistened black beneath my feet. I looked around and couldn't stop the yelp that escaped my throat. I covered my mouth and watched two nightmares conversing over a map spread on a massive wooden table.

One looked like a Destroyer, but larger than the ones I'd seen before. He was significantly taller with broad shoulders and a thick serpent body with black and brown scales. He wore a charcoal-colored silk tunic with gold embroidery on the edges and a massive gold pendant around his trunk of a neck. The pendant was strange, depicting a snake with rubies for eyes. It moved slowly and constantly, its body shaped like the number eight. Its endless slithering sent shivers down my spine.

I took a few steps forward and noticed his features—he'd once been a handsome man, but his square jaw and sharp cheeks were now ridden with black and brown scales, much like his lower body. His eyes were red—not just bloodshot but crimson even in his irises. His pupils dilated as he listened to the man standing next to him in front of the map.

I recognized the other guy as the Druid I'd seen getting tortured in my previous vision. He looked better now, but his deep-set eyes were dark, and his lips were a troubling shade of purple. His cheeks were sucked in, and his fingers trembled as he pointed at various locations on the map.

Despite the wails and cries for help oozing from the walls

around them, both seemed perfectly focused on their conversation.

"Marchosi, do not talk to me in riddles. I didn't spare your life to have to put up with your vague nuances," said the massive Destroyer. He crossed his arms. Two fingers caressed the moving snake pendant.

I quivered with disgust. He creeped the hell out of me.

"My apologies, Azazel. Allow me to better explain," the Druid named Marchosi replied.

My eyes grew wide as I realized I was standing in front of *him*. Azazel. The monster who wanted me locked in a glass ball, to serve him as he killed and pillaged his way through Eritopia. My inner-wolf growled instinctively. Oh, if only I could materialize in that room and turn into a werewolf so I could rip his throat out.

"Here and here are where the strangers were seen a few days ago, traveling up north through the Mohassian jungles." Marchosi pointed at two spots on the map, and Azazel followed his finger along the waxed paper.

"What sources do you have?"

"Solitary Sluaghs I keep in my league. I found them bodies in return for their services," the Druid replied. "They noticed unusual movements toward the northern mountains, and they followed the group, but they lost track of them in the woods."

"And you're sure they weren't just incubi wandering around?" Azazel asked, squinting his eyes at Marchosi.

"N-no, my liege," said the Druid with a trembling voice. "They were not Eritopian, at least two of them for sure weren't."

"Well, that's an interesting development. What about the other two?"

"From what I understood, one was a succubus, and the other was unidentifiable and blind."

It hit me then that Marchosi was referring to Serena, Jovi, Draven, and Anjani. They had been spotted during their trip to the Red Tribe. My stomach churned at the thought of them being spied on, but hearing the Druid say they'd lost them in the jungle gave me a minuscule sense of comfort. They hadn't tracked them all the way.

"We suspect there is a succubi settlement somewhere along those mountains," Marchosi continued. "But I've not been able to find it yet."

I took a few steps closer, my heart stuck in my throat. I wanted to get a better look at the map before my vision ended. But darkness enveloped me again too soon. I cursed between my teeth, unable to delay my leave.

* * *

I was standing between black walls again.

Damn!

I walked forward as the image before me came into focus. I was inside what looked like a dungeon. The ceiling arched above, while iron cages lined the walls on both sides. Creatures hissed and moaned, their crooked arms hanging limp between the bars.

Green flames flickered overhead, and I was able to recognize some of the prisoners. There were several…

Fae?

The fae were bruised and scratched all over, their once sparkling clothes now tattered and dirty. Some of them slept, while others wrestled against their shackles. I figured they were unable to use their ability to thin themselves and disappear due to Azazel's influence.

I felt so sorry for them, but I had to keep moving. I had to record as much as I could in my mind. I wondered how the fae had made it into Eritopia in the first place, but that was a question for Draven. There were endemic species in the dungeon, including dozens of succubi and a few incubi on the left. One of the incubi seemed dead, his gray eyes open wide and blank, silver blood dripping from his mouth as he lay on one side, motionless.

I instinctively covered my mouth with my hands to suppress a gasp. There were a couple of strange-looking women captive as well. They looked mostly human but had vibrant green and yellow scales covering their chests, legs, and arms. One of them yawned while leaning against the iron bars, and I could see her fangs and thin pink tongue, its tip split in two, reminding me of a snake. Was she a female Druid, perhaps? I'd have to ask Draven.

I jumped to the side, startled by noises behind me. I kept my mouth covered as I watched a Destroyer drag an incubus along the floor. He reached an empty cage and threw the new prisoner in there as if he were a sack of potatoes. The incubus landed inside with a thump and a groan, cursing under his breath.

As soon as the Destroyer locked the cage, the captive grabbed onto the bars and rattled them, startling the others. The Destroyer slammed a hand against the bars and hissed in response, and I took a few steps forward to get a better look.

I was surprised to see Sverik, Kristos' brother. I hadn't forgotten his handsome features from my previous vision. He'd been captured and imprisoned, despite what we'd heard about his father joining Azazel.

What is he doing here?

"You can't do this to me!" Sverik shouted at the Destroyer, prompting hisses and growls from the other prisoners.

"We can do whatever we want, little boy! You are insurance," the monster replied with a satisfied grin.

"We swore fealty to Azazel, both my father and I! There is no point in locking me up!"

"My lord needs to make sure that your grumpy old man obeys and doesn't think of turning his sword on us when things get rough. Blood is thicker than water," said the Destroyer and walked out.

I stood there for a minute, watching as Sverik struggled with the iron bars of his cage. His right eye was swollen and purple, and silver blood oozed from his lip. He must have put up quite the fight before getting dragged into the dungeon.

But what is this dungeon?

What is Azazel doing with all these creatures here?

SERENA

A few minutes into the session, I walked over to Aida's bedside. Draven's presence so close to me was draining me further, as I fought the urge to syphon off of him. I was so hungry that his delicious energy was breaking my focus.

I stood by Field's side, watching over Aida. Her eyes moved beneath her lids, and the shadow of a frown passed over her face once in a while. I wondered what she was seeing. I unwittingly leaned into Field's shoulder. I was feeling weaker and weaker.

Field looked at me, visibly concerned, and touched my forehead with the back of his hand. It felt cold against my skin, and I started to worry about the possibility that I was coming down with a fever. I was more susceptible to illness if I didn't feed as a sentry.

"You look pale, Serena," Field said slowly. "When's the last time you syphoned?"

"When we first got here." I gave him a weak smile.

"Damnit, girl. You know you can syphon off me and Jovi whenever you need a pick-me-up." He took hold of my hand.

I nodded slowly and allowed myself to open up and draw his energy in. It felt like a warm summer breeze rushing through my veins. I closed my eyes and watched the bluish green ribbons of energy sizzle from his body to mine. I felt what he felt in that moment—concern and uncertainty over what our future had in store for us and a blossoming warmth in his chest every time he looked at Aida. I felt the tension in his stomach from being close to her. I saw flickers of Aida in the back of my head, projected by Field's mind.

He cleared his throat, and I pulled myself from him, realizing I was digging too far into his soul. I felt invigorated all of a sudden. Strength returned to my legs. I took a deep breath and thanked him for his support.

Before he could respond, his gaze passed over Aida and froze. His eyes widened in shock. I looked down and gasped at the sight of ink black runes fluttering across her entire body, moving beneath her skin.

"Draven," I managed to call out. "There's something going on with Aida."

"What's wrong?" I heard him ask from behind.

"Runes... I can see runes on her skin... They're moving across her body, but they are clear as day!"

"You need to draw as many of them as you can, Serena, in the succession in which they appear," Draven replied. "Check the cabinet by the door. I keep writing tools in there for various observations during my experiments."

Field immediately rummaged through a drawer and found an old notebook with off-white paper and a few pieces of charcoal. He brought them over and tore a few pages out for me. We started copying as many runes as we could.

"Experiments?" Field asked, an eyebrow raised as he followed the symbols flickering across Aida's collarbones.

"This isn't just a treatment room. It's also where I study different plants and animals. I've had a lot of spare time on my hands," Draven said bluntly.

"Of course you did," came my sarcastic remark. "Doctor Frankenstein would be proud."

"Who's that?" he asked.

"Never mind," I muttered, as I hurriedly sketched the runes.

"Are you writing everything down?" Draven asked.

"We're trying to cover as much as we can," Field replied. "But a lot of them vanish and re-emerge on different sides."

"What *are* these runes anyway?" I frowned over Aida's left arm, trying to make out the combinations of lines, points, and geometrical shapes forming each symbol. I wondered if she could feel them at all in her state.

"They're the ancient language of the Oracles. It holds millennia of wisdom and knowledge of Eritopia. It often relates to what visions the Oracles are having in that precise moment and is usually more helpful than the visions themselves," Draven explained. "One Oracle might just see a tree on a hill, for example, but the runes might talk about the bones of the Ancients buried beneath, bones which, if found, can be ground into a fine powder and used for extremely powerful magic, like my father found out during one of Elissa's visions."

I kept writing the sequences down. Aida's chest moved slowly with each even breath.

Vita

I stood in front of a wide, open space on a terrace made of black limestone and marble. Tall arches rested on slim pillars that framed the circular plateau all around me. The sky above was a dark shade of pink as the sun drifted beneath the horizon to my left.

I turned around and found myself facing the large glass sphere where the Nevertide Oracle floated unconsciously. Her long fingers slid along the glass. Her white eyes opened wide, as if staring directly at me.

"Vita."

Her voice echoed in my head. This was the second time that I was in a vision of the future and the Oracle could somehow feel me there. It was just as creepy as the first time. I heard noises behind me, grunts and gasps and familiar voices getting closer.

I froze when I watched Aida, Phoenix, and a future version of myself being dragged up to the terrace in iron shackles by three Destroyers. My heart jumped into my throat, and my stomach tightened. Azazel followed behind them wearing a satisfied grin on his face.

A serpent made of gold with small ruby eyes slithered in a figure eight hanging on a chain around his neck. The lower half of his body was massive. I stepped closer to him for a better look. He commanded the Destroyers to put all of us in three glass spheres filled with what looked like water. They were mounted beneath three nearby arches, waiting to be occupied by Oracles.

I wanted to shout, to shoot fire at them, to rip their eyes out with my bare hands. I felt consumed by the rage of feeling useless before this horrifying scene. Phoenix's eyes were red and swollen, and most of his face was severely bruised. He must have fought the Destroyers. He must have tried to stop this from happening. Aida was passed out. Her feet dragged along the ground. One of the monsters pulled her up like she weighed less than a pillow.

Azazel muttered something, and one of the spheres opened up on one side without spilling over, enough for the Destroyer to shove her inside before it sealed itself back. I watched Aida's body as it turned and twitched helplessly, the fluid filling her lungs until she stilled. I watched my future self cry and scream out, begging Azazel to stop. A Destroyer's arm nearly crushed my torso with his grip.

"This is what you get for being naughty little children," Azazel hissed at us.

I shivered as I watched the Destroyers put Phoenix and my future self into the other two spheres. The liquid filled our lungs until we stopped moving.

"Vita, there isn't much time left," I heard the Nevertide Oracle in my head.

I couldn't face her again. My chest was about to explode from the grief of watching myself and my friends in those spheres, destined for an eternity of misery and imprisonment. Aida floated slowly on one side, enough for me to see her face. Her eyes opened wide—blank and white—and runes emerged and slid across her pale skin.

Azazel laughed with great satisfaction, and I knew that all three of us were experiencing visions against our will.

"Vita, listen to me," the Nevertide Oracle called out to me again.

But before I could look at her again, I watched Azazel slither up to her and caress the glass between them with one hand.

"You wonderful, wonderful creature," he hissed at her. "I wouldn't have gotten the whole set of Oracles without your…assistance. So, thank you, my darling. You've been a great asset!"

I froze at his statement, then looked at the Oracle. She looked so miserable, but what did it mean? Was that real suffering or just the guilt she felt for having betrayed us all?

My anger burned like fire until everything went dark. I wanted to stay longer, to see more and find out whether she really had played a part in our capture or whether she'd just been an unwilling pawn in Azazel's game, but my vision faded and took me deeper into the future.

* * *

The darkness dissipated, and another place came into focus. The black stone architecture made me think I was still somewhere in Azazel's citadel. Everything exuded suffering and doom. A nearby window revealed that the sky was a dark purple now, riddled with black and gray clouds that occasionally glowed from the electrical storms they carried.

My gaze immediately fixed on Serena, and my heart stopped for a moment. She was slightly older, her eyes wearing decades of experience more than the Serena I knew. Her skin was tanned, and her body was clad in black leather and silver armor, reminding me of Anjani and her warrior succubi sisters.

Her hands were tied behind her back. Her torso was chained and hung from the tall ceiling above a massive fire pit. Green flames licked at her naked feet. She kept pulling them back to avoid the burns. She must have been in a lot of pain, but she didn't show it.

I looked around to see the rest of the hall, square and spacious with massive torches mounted on the walls.

Azazel stood by the edge of the fire pit, hissing with delight as he enjoyed the heat. His serpent tail twitched, and his fingers caressed the moving serpent medallion hung around his neck.

I saw two massive doors open into the room. In came two Destroyers dragging Draven along in heavy black chains. There were symbols carved into the cuffs, and it made me wonder whether they had some binding spell that forced the Druid into submission. My heart twisted at the sight of Serena crying out his name.

"Draven, no! What did you do?!"

The Destroyers pulled him closer to the fire. Azazel slithered around the pit to get a better look at his face. His grin made me nauseous. I took a few deep breaths to keep myself under control, telling myself that this was still in the future, that it hadn't happened yet, and that I would do everything I could to stop it from happening altogether.

"I'm here, as you can see," Draven said to Azazel. His tone oozed sarcasm as the Destroyers forced him to stand.

His ankle was swollen, and blood drizzled from his temple, where he'd been recently hit. Nevertheless, he leaned into his other leg, unwavering in front of Azazel, who took his chin in his scaly hand and turned his head to one side, a pensive look on his face. I could see black and brown scales spreading out from Azazel's neck onto his cheeks on both sides. His eyes glistened red.

"Hmm. You do take after your father," Azazel mused, then pulled the Druid's hair painfully to one side, jerking his head.

Draven winced but kept a straight face.

"I'm here, as per the terms of our agreement," he said, his voice low.

I froze, as did Serena, who stilled against her restraints, her cheeks red from the flames below. Tears welled in her eyes, and I understood then that she had developed feelings for the Druid. It broke my heart, but I kept my composure and continued watching the exchange.

"Draven, what did you do?" Serena cried out.

"What I had to do to keep you alive," he replied, his gaze softening as their eyes met.

"No, no, no, Draven, no! You can't! We need you! Eritopia needs you! I'm not important. I'm not worth your sacrifice. Don't!"

Azazel roared with laughter as he snapped his fingers, and the chain keeping Serena attached to the ceiling moved and threw her backward against a wall. She hit the floor with a thud, coughing and struggling to stand.

"When will you understand, Serena, that you are worth everything to me?" Draven said before shifting his attention back to Azazel. "She lives. You guaranteed it."

"I'm a Druid of my word," Azazel hissed and grinned, snapping his fingers again.

Another Destroyer emerged from the darkness and dragged Serena out of the hall, despite her flailing legs and screams.

"Draven! Draven!"

The vision faded into darkness again, but Draven's response echoed anyway.

"You're not a Druid anymore, Azazel, you're a monster."

* * *

I drifted further into time. This was immediately clear from the moment the image before my eyes came into focus. The sky was black and heavy with thick clouds above Eritopia. The thousands of acres of lush jungles had been burned down and stripped to charred trunks and blackened dust. I was on the same platform where I had seen our capture and the Nevertide Oracle, but the arches had been torn down, and rubble was spread at my feet.

I stood above a lifeless wasteland on the edge of the circular terrace. Glass spheres were shattered, shards scattered around. A pang in my heart drew my focus to the center of the scene, where I found Azazel.

His serpent tail flicked around, his clawed hands digging deep into Draven's chest. I cried out, but I couldn't hear my own voice. Instead, I heard Serena's scream. She was on her knees, in shackles, held down by a Destroyer.

A golden light poured out of Draven as Serena cried out his name, her face pale with devastation. Azazel was feeding off the Druid's energy from what I could tell, and I could see his body light up from within, like an incandescent lightbulb. Azazel laughed as he drained him of his life force.

I saw Phoenix, Aida, and myself lumped on one side, our arms tied behind us, runes flickering over our bodies, and our eyes wide and white. I looked over the edge of the platform and noticed another level below, larger and with wide, circular steps descending toward the lowest terrace, many miles down. Hundreds of incubi and succubi lay on the terraces and the stairs, their bodies limp and lifeless.

"This is the perfect recipe for success! A Druid's life force can be truly extraordinary!" Azazel barked as he continued to draw power from Draven.

The Druid turned pale, the last flickers of life leaving his gray eyes. His gaze settled on Serena. The shadow of a smile passed over his face.

She cried, tears streaming down her cheeks. I felt my own eyes burn, but I couldn't look away. I couldn't leave them there. I had to make sure I could stop this before it became a distant probability.

I walked forward to get a better look at Azazel's claws piercing Draven's flesh. Blood dripped from the Druid's wounds while his once tanned skin lost its color.

"You see, Serena," Azazel said to her, his eyes burning red, "I need a lot of energy to find another world to conquer. Eritopia's weak now. It can no longer sustain my grandeur. I need something more. I am a king in need of a kingdom!"

"You're a sick bastard, drunk on your own power!" Serena barked at him between hiccups, while she continued to struggle against her restraints and the Destroyer's firm grip.

"You know what? Just because you've been such a pain in my hide from the moment you and your precious little Oracle friends got here, I think I'll just go ahead and wipe your kind off the face of…what do you call it? Earth?" Azazel grinned.

He pulled his arms back. Draven dropped motionless to the floor. Serena's shrill scream pierced through the sky and tore me apart. I moved, so I wouldn't have to see his eyes open wide, staring lifelessly at her.

Azazel's claws were glazed in scarlet blood. His skin glimmered gold where it hadn't been tainted by black scales. He straightened his back and tore his white silk shirt off, revealing his bare chest.

"Just because you've been such a nuisance, such a loud little insect constantly ruining my work, I'll show you what it's really like to irk a god like me! Your Druid's just the beginning, my darling!" He laughed maniacally and started scratching runes across his chest, his claws drawing blood with each scratch.

Serena froze, swallowing back tears and watching him in disbelief. She recognized the ritual that Azazel was performing, and so did I. Draven had done the same when he took us to see the Daughters. Where were the Daughters in all of this?

"The Daughters will never let you leave!" Serena shot back, as if reading my non-present mind somehow.

Azazel chuckled as he finished cutting the runes into his flesh. "The Daughters are gone, my darling. Haven't you noticed?"

A moment of silence followed. Then, Azazel clapped his hands once, and the golden light inside of him expanded outward, as if a star had just been ignited for the first time.

"What…what are you talking about?" Serena's voice trembled

from across the terrace.

The light shone brighter until it was a blinding white, as if we were being swallowed by a nebula. As everything was engulfed by it, Azazel's words thundered, hurting my ears.

"The Daughters have left, Serena! They've abandoned Eritopia, and now, so will we! I'm taking my army to your Earth and burning it all down, and you're coming along, my darling. I'm going to make you watch as I destroy everything you hold dear."

Serena's cry was the last thing I was able to make out as pure hot whiteness glazed me. I felt like I was disintegrating.

Phoenix

I walked through the jungle. Giant purple trees with gnarly branches reached out above, their dark oval leaves obscuring my view of an orange sky. It was dusk, by the looks of it. I followed a narrow trail that snaked through the forest. Swamp canals ran along both sides. Where there weren't trees, thick mauve foliage, and bundles of dark green shrubs, there were steady streams of murky water riddled with fast-moving shadows.

Little red lights flickered across the water like fireflies. Birds sang overhead. Branches broke, and leaves rustled somewhere behind me. I looked over my shoulder and saw a small figure, about as tall as Vita, emerge from the forest.

The creature wore a dark brown hood, clutching a black leather bag in its skinny arms. It tripped and fell to the ground. A soft voice cursed. It was a woman, I realized, and stopped to get a better look.

She stood up and pulled the hood back to better see ahead. She looked right through me. Her hair was rich, black, and braided with black and white feathers. Her skin was pale, almost as white as marble, and decorated with thousands of tiny green bead piercings mounted in straight vertical lines along her limbs. She was thin, with bony ankles and wrists, and she wore shiny rows of red beads on her forearms and calves. She looked young, but the dirt on her sharp-edged face made it difficult for me to tell more than that.

She walked right through me, and I decided to follow her. Clearly, she was the reason I was having this vision. I walked behind her as she struggled with the heavy load hanging from her shoulder.

We soon reached an open space, semicircular in form, with a tall limestone mountain wall occupying the straight edge. The grass at our feet was purple like the trees around us. I watched the woman as she approached the wall, looking up. The surface seemed carved with giant faces, simple slanted eyes, thin lines for mouths, and an abundance of red vines climbing and spreading across.

"I'm here to see Klibi," the woman shouted at no one in particular.

A moment passed before the ground started to shake. I froze as I watched the limestone wall tremble and crackle with life. The forms I'd seen sculpted into it emerged from the mountain, their features far more pronounced. They rumbled as they stood up, vines still attached to their legs.

They were massive stone giants, and I wondered if these were the Dearghs that Anjani had told us about. One of them took a step forward and looked down at the tiny woman—she was microscopic in comparison.

"What is a swamp witch doing so far away from home?" The giant's voice thundered through the clearing.

"I told you, I'm here to speak to Klibi. Now," the woman commanded.

I moved closer in order to get a better look. I had heard about swamp witches from Serena's account of their visit to the Red Tribe during breakfast, and this was a unique opportunity to see one up close, since they were presumed to be extinct.

"What business do you have with Klibi, little one?"

"I am here on behalf of my entire coven, Deargh. I seek Klibi's help to protect our magic from Azazel. You must have heard by now that he's been starting wars against the eastern citadels of the incubi. Agoris has already fallen, and he has captured three of my sisters," the witch explained, her voice low, full, and warm.

I stood before five enormous Dearghs and a small but fearless swamp witch. The giants stepped aside, making room for her to walk forward and past the wide opening left in the wall.

I followed closely as she climbed up a stony ridge until she reached a red marble plateau just a few feet above the ground. The view was different from up there. I could see the dark purple tree crowns undulating below, hiding the water streams and even the trail I'd followed up there. The wind brushed through the tall purple grass.

The sound of stones cracking made me turn around to see another Deargh standing in front of the swamp witch. The woman bowed respectfully and pulled something out of her leather pack. It was a book, from what I could see, bound in a dark animal hide with strange symbols embroidered on the cover. She handed it to the giant, who took it with two massive fingers, as if he were picking up a little fly.

"Klibi, we need your help," the swamp witch addressed the Deargh.

"What is this?" Klibi asked, his voice powerful and heavy.

"It is one of our three books of Knowledge. I need you to keep it safe," she replied.

"Why come to us for this?"

"Because you are the strongest of the Dearghs, and Azazel wouldn't dare attack you, not even with his monstrous Druids and their poisoned arrows. He's amassing great power in the east, and he's been hunting my kind down. He's after our magic, and we cannot, under any circumstances, let him have it. You know very well what we are capable of, and Azazel must not wield such power. It would be the end of Eritopia."

The Deargh thought about this for a while. Then, he nodded and stood.

"That is fine, little witch," he replied, on a slightly gentler tone.

"You've helped us in the past, and we will return the favor."

The witch nodded her appreciation.

"Thank you, Klibi," she said. "Rest assured that you are doing Eritopia a great service by protecting this book."

"When will you be back for it?"

"I don't know," she sighed, and I could almost sense the sorrow in her voice. "I may never come back for it. I would rather die than lead Azazel to it. He's closing in on our coven, and there are traitors among the incubi. It's how he's been able to kill my sisters. We never see him coming."

Klibi nodded, looking at the book, tiny in the palm of his hand.

"What do you want us to do with it, then?" he asked.

"Keep it safe for as long as time flows in this world. Someday, if I don't come back for it, someone else will. I don't know who, for I cannot see into the future, but someone is likely to rise against Azazel, strong and bold and ready to take him down. Only a worthy fighter must gain access to this book."

"I understand, little witch. I will make sure that your knowledge ends only in good and pure hands. You have my word."

I had so many questions for the Druid, but in the meantime, I was surprised and intrigued by how detailed and lengthy this vision was. I'd only had snippets of the past before and been unable to understand much from them.

This, on the other hand, was quite an elaborate memory of a time long gone. Before I could move around and see or hear more, however, the image before me blurred, and I was enveloped by a familiar darkness.

* * *

Not long after that, I heard different voices.

"Almus, what is this?" A husky, feminine voice shot through my consciousness.

The darkness around me dissolved into a different scene, bathed in an abundance of warm, orange light. I looked around and realized that I was inside a tent. It was a conical shape with loose seams and animal furs padding the floor.

It was spacious, and delicate translucent layers of red and white fabric were hung overhead, pinned from one side to the other and gently falling down like soft curtains. They served a decorative purpose and contrasted nicely with the amber light and black furs. Various swords and shields were gathered on one side next to a massive wooden chest with metallic hinges.

At the far end, opposite from the entrance, was a large slab of black stone that resembled obsidian. Its surface was smooth, seemingly polished to perfection. In front of it stood a young succubus, her skin glimmering silver, and a man. He wore the 1800s attire I'd already grown accustomed to at the mansion, and the name Almus instantly rang a bell. He was Draven's father.

I took a few steps closer to see both of them better.

"It's a passage stone," he said to the succubus.

I couldn't help but marvel at her beauty, which was eerily similar to Anjani's. Her long black hair spilled over her shoulders in an abundance of curls. Her eyes were wide with swirls of gold and emerald, and her lips invited a man to taste them for an eternity. Her curves were equally appealing, wrapped in leathers and slim belts made of gold and encrusted with precious rubies. A massive sword hung lazily from her hip, cradled in a beautifully crafted scabbard with heavy gold ornaments, complete with artful filigree.

She may have been designed by nature to seduce, but judging by her firm muscles and menacing weapons, this succubus was also a fearsome killing machine.

"What is it doing here?" she asked him, a smile tugging at the corner of her mouth.

"I'm gifting it to you, Hansa."

And all the pieces came into place. No wonder she looked familiar! I'd heard about Hansa, Anjani's sister and chief of the Red Tribe. My mind immediately flew back to Jovi. I'd noticed how he looked at Anjani when he thought no one could see him— dumbstruck and fascinated. I couldn't blame him, really. Looking at this creature in particular, he'd had every reason to find himself ensnared.

Judging by how Draven's father was looking at Hansa, he seemed to be suffering from the same affliction. The flickers in his gray eyes were not reflections of the tent's light, but embers of attraction. The succubus seemed to have quite the effect on the Druid.

"It connects this place to a hidden cave beneath my mansion, which is under the protection of the Daughters' shield," he explained. "It's for us to communicate and make sure the books are safe. The swamp witches are all gone, but we still have their priceless heritage. If something ever happens to either of us, the other can use the passage stone to retrieve them."

Hansa smiled and caressed the side of his face. The Druid leaned into her touch, closing his eyes. I was beginning to feel a little awkward and hoped that my vision wasn't going to show me something I'd regret seeing.

"Thank you, Almus. That is very thoughtful of you," she replied gently. "How does it work?"

"It needs your blood. It will only take you to a place with another stone, a place you have already seen. You shouldn't risk it otherwise. I've heard horrible stories of its misuse."

"Then you need to show me where your mansion is, darling," Hansa smiled and closed the distance between them, bringing her face barely an inch from his. "You know where I live, but I don't know where you live, and I think we're past the stage in our relationship where we can keep such secrets from each other."

Almus laughed lightly and sealed her lips with a kiss. I noticed that he held a book in his right hand—one I had seen before, identical to that given to Klibi by the swamp witch.

"At the next full moon, I will show you, Hansa. I promise. I just need to prepare Draven for this. You must understand," he said.

Were they in some kind of relationship? Was he about to break the news to his son? I had so many questions for Draven. It felt like watching a drama on TV, and I personally knew one of the protagonists. I held back a chuckle as Hansa took a step back, wavering a little before the Druid.

"Are you sure you want me to meet him, Almus?" she asked.

"It's been a long time since that boy has seen anyone other than Elissa. He needs to experience some kind of change in his life. He gets so lonely, Hansa."

"As long as you think it's the right thing to do, I won't mind. I'm already too deep in this to back out. I'm so close to breaking tribal traditions." She smiled and kissed him gently on one cheek, intentionally close to the corner of his mouth.

"Neither of us saw this coming, Hansa. You surprised me," he replied and held the book up between them.

They were both trying not to tear the other's clothes off, judging by their heavy breathing and bedroom eyes. I took a step back then, not sure if I wanted to see what happened next. Whereas previous visions had ended too soon, this one sure seemed to take its time.

"I'll take this back to the mansion tonight. Make sure you hide yours as well. I must not know where it is," Almus said slowly.

"They're all dead, aren't they?" Hansa asked, her gaze fixed on the book, darkened by sadness.

Almus nodded. "They were betrayed."

Before I could hear more, darkness poured over my eyes once more.

Typical.

When I wanted it to end it sure didn't rush me out of there, but when I wanted to stay, it immediately pulled me out. I'd have to work harder to try to control these visions.

* * *

The image came into focus again, painted in vibrant strokes of crude green and electric pinks and oranges beneath a deep blue sky. Long strings of pale orange sky ran across, from east to west, as the giant sun slowly began its descent.

I stood on top of a mountain. It was so tall that I could see the rest of the world curve gently at the horizon. The view was breathtaking, and I soaked it all in slowly—a stunning display of lush jungles with young trees that barely rose from the tall grass and sharp hills that had yet to be eroded by the passage of time. Volcanoes spurted bright orange lava in the distance, and rivers flowed wildly across the land.

A peculiar crackle prompted me to turn around. I realized then that I was on the very peak of the mountain. My feet were inches from the edge. Below me, a deep crevice split the mountain in half. Two sharp tips of white marble rose around a pool of hot water. The water climbed as high as the walls allowed before spilling outward from the low side of the crevice and cascading down the mountain.

The water was a dark pink. Its luscious surface reminded me of the new Daughter's hair. It held the same fascinating hues of red and fuchsia, like paint had been poured in it and swirled around.

I heard the crackle again, but it took me a while to identify its source. The pink water was bubbling up on the surface with white foamy rings expanding one after another, traveling with the ripples.

The wind blew strong at that altitude. I could tell from the way the handful of purple shrubs nearby bent with it. It whistled and swished between the white marble peaks, creating a pleasant acoustic effect in combination with the sound of water dropping for thousands of yards along the mountain.

I bent over slowly to get a better view of the pink water. I could see my reflection in it, barely a stick figure at that height. The water trembled, and a white egg emerged from below. I stilled, realizing that it looked eerily familiar. It was a large shell with a pearly white glaze and thin red veins spread out on its surface.

It floated around for a while until the bubbles gently pushed it toward a flat sliver of white marble onto which the egg rolled quietly. The pink water lapped at the narrow shore. I got down on my knees, not sure whether I could do anything else from that angle. I had yet to explore the physics of my visions, but given all the rugged ridges of marble that waited below, I didn't want to risk it.

The last rays of sunshine passed over the egg, throwing shades of amber and rose against its shimmering shell. I stayed there for a while, wondering what else I would see. I didn't want to draw any conclusion just yet, not based solely on the resemblance of that egg.

Before I could formulate another thought, the shell cracked, and I held my breath. After a few more pushes, it hatched, and out of it came a marvelous creature—one I knew in my heart was exactly who I had suspected. It was a Daughter of Eritopia, so young and pure, with pale skin and reddish pink hair and the same electric violet eyes that I'd become so fond of back at the mansion.

She looked around with a dazed look on her face. Her attention was then drawn to the pink water, which pushed out a few more eggs. It dawned on me that I was watching the birth of the Daughters of Eritopia at the beginning of time.

One by one, they hatched from their eggs. Seven of them, similar in appearance, clearly sisters. Their hair flowed straight down their backs in shades of fiery red and pink. Their eyes burned bright like violet flames. Their lips were soft and full, drawn in beautiful cupid's bows. Their skin was opalescent, delicate veins slightly visible underneath.

They looked at each other, gently brushing their fingers through each other's hair with genuine fascination. They were discovering themselves as sisters. The Daughters then looked around, taking it all in. From where they stood, they could see the white marble walls of the crevice that held them, the pink water at their feet, the darkening sky above, and perhaps glimpses of the crude world where the peak split in two.

They listened to the sound of the water like I did and then nodded to one another, as if they understood something that I didn't. The Daughters walked up to the marble wall behind them and placed their ears against it, closing their eyes and taking deep breaths.

I then realized what this entire vision was about. I was standing on Mount Agrith. No one had left the Daughters' eggs on top of it; Eritopia had created them. They were born with a clear understanding of the world that surrounded them. As they listened to the water and the natural elements, they were able to understand Eritopia itself.

These weren't goddesses as we'd suspected. They were not creators. They were so deeply tied to Eritopia that the world itself resonated through their bodies and their powers. It must have been the source of their incredible abilities. They walked around that shore for a while, listening to every sound and nodding their approval, as if Eritopia was talking to them.

It made me wonder: what if they could actually communicate with it? What if Eritopia spoke to the Daughters?

Aida

I opened my eyes to find the familiar dirty plaster of the basement ceiling above peeling here and there from the humidity. I sat up with a jolt, my mind flooded with memories of my visions. I had so much to tell the Druid!

My skin tickled all over, and when I looked down I saw black runes fluttering across my chest and limbs. A heatwave burned through me, and I let out a short but pained scream. I had hoped I'd never see those things on me again.

I swatted away at them as if fending off thousands of spiders and cursed under my breath until a pair of strong arms took hold of me. Field's voice poured into my ear, calming me down.

"It's okay, Aida, it's okay. I've got you," he said gently.

I couldn't help but whimper, looking at my arms with sheer horror.

"Get them off me! This is so creepy!" I yelped, warm tears streaming down my cheeks.

He held me close, and I could feel his solid frame molded against mine. The runes started to fade, as if washed away by the rain. One by one, they disappeared, and I felt like I could finally breathe again. I sighed with relief, thankful that they didn't seem permanent, and leaned my head against Field's chest.

A few moments later, I was stable enough to notice Serena and Draven standing by my bedside. Serena took my hand in hers and squeezed it, giving me silent assurance that everything was going to be okay. But I knew, deep in my heart, that wasn't exactly true. After all, I had just seen runes on my body again, and I clearly couldn't chalk it up to a hallucination anymore.

"How are you feeling?" Serena asked me, concern in her blue eyes.

"I would say I'm doing just peachy, but that would not be true," I snapped.

She didn't say anything. I knew she didn't deserve to be in my line of fire.

"Sorry," I mumbled and relaxed in Field's arms. He thankfully didn't let go of me.

"Unfortunately, the runes are a part of who you are now," Draven said, not making me feel any better. "But from what I've read about the Oracles and what I know from Elissa, the transformation process that you're going through seems to be different from the usual. That might be of some comfort, I hope."

"By different than usual you mean I've not yet gone fully blind or lost my lady parts?" I couldn't help the snappy tone. Frustration dominated my state of mind.

Draven took a deep breath, his lips drawn in a thin, flat line. He didn't deserve it either, but I canceled that thought out when I remembered that he'd brought us to Eritopia in the first place. He'd have to put up with my snappy tone if it provided me with some catharsis. I'd earned that right.

"What did you see?" he asked, wise enough to not engage me on the positive aspects of my Oracle symptoms.

I told him about the first vision, describing the vivid jungle, the succubi, the Dearghs, and the conversation regarding the volcanoes. He nodded slowly as I recounted the moving stone giants and the way they used the volcano fires to travel from one clan to another.

"Is there anything there that helps us?" I asked at the end.

"Absolutely." Draven nodded. "This doesn't just confirm that Hansa is already busy holding up her end of the bargain, which is very good news, but it also confirms my suspicion that the Dearghs had no idea why their volcanoes are dying out. I've been tracking the phenomenon for decades now. It's good that they know now. It will be their incentive to rise up against Azazel.

"After all," he continued, "they might all be gentle servants of nature, but they don't take kindly to cheating at the expense of their own kind. The way the Dearghs travel is new to me. I'm guessing they have no problem with lava, since their core is pure fire, but I can't help but wonder whether we could take advantage of this method of transportation for ourselves."

"What, like move from one volcano to another through fire and lava?" I made sure sarcasm dripped from each word.

"With a protection spell powerful enough, we could probably do exactly that," the Druid replied, ignoring my tone of voice. "Did you see anything else?"

"Yeah, it was another set of three visions, basically. I think it might be a pattern," I replied.

"It makes sense. There are three Oracles, each with three visions each. There must be some significance in this. Tell me more."

I chronicled my second vision of Azazel and the Druid I'd seen tortured before. I described their conversation over a map of the northern jungles. I made sure not to miss any details, including the moving serpent made of gold with small ruby eyes.

"The Druid's name was Marchosi," I added.

Draven stilled for a second, then nodded. I noticed the tension in his jaw, and judging by Serena's expression, so did she.

"Who's Marchosi?" she asked.

"Marchosi was once a very close friend of my father's. They were raised together, educated by the same Druid Masters. I didn't think he'd still be alive," the Druid replied. "But his presence in this war is extremely detrimental to my plans. He has plenty of spies of his own throughout Eritopia, as he was once in charge of diplomatic affairs between the citadels and had to make sure that there would be no unpleasant or bloody surprises for his convoys. The worst part about his involvement is that he might know about my existence, although I'm not certain of it. It's something I'll have to consider going forward."

"The fact that Azazel doesn't know about you and this place has been at the core of everything we've done so far," Serena said. "What will we do if he finds out?"

"Even if he does find out, he won't be able to find us here. We are under the Daughters' protection. The shield is impervious to any attack, and we are virtually invisible beneath it, as you know already. The problem isn't that he'd know about the mansion. He can't do anything about it anyway. It's that if he finds out I exist, he'll add me to his list of enemies, and that means I'll be a new chapter in his strategy to gain full control of Eritopia. When your enemy knows who you are, you are that much more vulnerable."

The Druid straightened his back and nodded, as if having just found his resolve.

"It's fine, we'll cross that bridge when we get there," he continued. "Tell me about your third vision, Aida."

Feeling as if I'd saved the best for last, I told Draven about the dungeon and all the creatures held captive there.

"There were dozens of them, from all walks of life. There were even some fae with tattered formal dresses, as if they'd been snatched in the middle of a banquet. There were plenty of incubi and succubi and I think some female Druids, if you have those." I remembered the beautiful women with exotic scales, serpent tongues, and fangs.

"I don't think there are any left, from what I know. What did they look like?"

I described them in full detail, down to the color of their scales and their eyes.

"Those are Lamias," Draven explained. "They're often confused with female Druids, but they never take the full form of a serpent. They look like what you might consider to be regular women, but they have a developing snake skin that gradually covers their entire body. Once they're fully covered, they shed it and emerge with a different appearance and different physical features, as if they are different women altogether."

"That sounds pretty cool, actually," Serena mused.

"They only feed on incubus or succubus flesh," Draven added.

"Oh. I take that back, then."

"Many millennia ago, they were once relatives of the Druid species, like cousins, you might say. But they were banished to the darkest corners of the jungle for their horrible appetite. I can tell you more about them later," the Druid said, then turned his attention back on me. "Go on, Aida."

"Yeah, so there were all kinds of creatures in that dungeon, and judging by the color of the walls and the lights, they were in the same building as Azazel—black stone and green fires. They all had heavy iron shackles around their wrists and ankles and were stuck in individual locked cages."

"Shackles *and* cages. Only one of the two is used for imprisonment. The other must be a suppressor of the captive's abilities, like the fae, for example," Draven concluded, then waited for me to continue.

"Then I saw a Destroyer come in, dragging an incubus and throwing him inside one of those cages. Thing is, I've seen that incubus before. It was Kristos' brother, and he'd been severely beaten."

"Sverik is a prisoner of Azazel? How could that be? His father swore his allegiance to Azazel," the Druid asked.

"He was telling the Destroyer the same thing," I explained. "But then the Destroyer said that Azazel had decided to keep him caged to make sure that his father didn't think of doing something stupid, like turning against them."

Draven nodded and crossed his arms on his chest, bringing one hand up to support his chin while he processed the new information. I further relaxed into Field's arms. His heart beat against the back of my head. With everything going on, his presence seemed to be my anchor to sanity.

"Azazel must be holding all those creatures there, including Sverik, for specific reasons, then. Knowing him and his strategies so far, I'm willing to bet these reasons include blackmail, ransom, and even experiments, since he draws his dark magic from living beings. He uses the volcanoes for high-powered spells during war campaigns and to corrupt his Destroyers, but the creatures are the core source for his black arts," Draven concluded.

I felt sorry for all those creatures. A pang dug into my heart. Imprisonment seemed like a fate worse than death when your captor was Azazel. They must've felt hopeless in there, while the life was gradually snuffed out of them, as if they were just batteries that could be discarded once he was done with them.

The more I thought of the vision of the fae stuck in those cages, with their blank gazes and livid complexions, the more determined I was to help bring this half-snake ass down. By comparison, the disappearing runes on my skin seemed trivial. At least I wasn't shackled in some filthy basement at the whims of a megalomaniac with no honor or respect for life.

PHOENIX

I woke up with a start and immediately sat up, as if pushed out of my vision and right back into reality. I shook my head and blinked several times, taking in my surroundings and the voices around me. The dark green tiles below, the dim lights from the oil lamps, the cool air, and the off-white sheets of my bed immediately fell into place. I was in the basement.

My eyes caught some kind of movement on my body, and when I looked down, I froze at the sight of thousands of black runes moving across my skin in strings along my torso and arms. I tried rubbing them off as if they were the ballpoint pen smudges I used to get back at school in The Shade, but they lingered for a while before dissipating on their own.

"What the hell?!" I exclaimed and looked around in a panic.

Jovi stood by my side with paper and charcoal in his hands. Scribbles that resembled my runes were jotted down on the paper with jagged lines and rushed curves.

"It's okay, Phoenix. Look. They're gone." Serena rushed over to my side and hugged me.

"Were those runes?!" I asked, unwilling to calm down just yet.

"Yes. You've all been covered with them during your visions," Jovi explained and showed me the notes he'd made.

I heard a gasp and the sound of bare feet hitting the tiles to my right and felt arms wrap around me. It was the Daughter, who held me as tightly as she could. Her arms were warm and soothing and calmed me. I took deep breaths, my face submerged in her long reddish pink hair. She was soft and hot against my skin. Her cheek rubbed against my jaw. I felt my stubble scratching her, but she didn't seem to mind.

I looked to my left and saw Aida sitting up in her bed, leaning against Field. She gave me an understanding look and nodded with a faint smile. I felt my body relax, both from the Daughter's embrace and Aida's reassuring expression.

"We tried to write down as many of them as possible during your visions," Serena said.

"Do we know what they mean?" I asked, running my fingers through my hair.

"No. Unfortunately, the Oracles could never translate them outside their visions," Draven replied, inching toward my bed from

Aida's side.

The Daughter threw a glance over the notes in Jovi's hand.

"I know what they mean," she said, once again stunning us all.

"You do?" Draven asked, and she nodded. "How can you tell?" he asked.

"I'm not sure," she shrugged. "But they all represent words that I recognize. I've always known that language."

"Well, that certainly adds to your purpose in this particular dynamic," the Druid responded, his tone soft enough to sound like genuine appreciation. "I must kindly ask that you assist us with their translation afterward if you can."

"Will it help Phoenix?"

My heart thumped at the sound of her question. Everything seemed to revert to me as far as her decisions were concerned.

"It will help him, and it will help all of us," Draven replied.

"I will help you translate them, then."

Serena held my hand. Our eyes met for a moment—I needed my sister near me. The clarity that her presence gave me was undeniable. Soon enough, all the jitters scattered away, and I was left with an accurate set of visions.

"We need to talk, Druid," I said to him, eager to get the images of the past out of the way. I had so many questions for him, some inappropriate and possibly infuriating, I realized. I stifled a grin. "I had three visions of the past."

"Alas, the pattern repeats itself," Draven mused. "Please, do tell."

I told him about the first one, involving the woman I had seen with what I assumed were Dearghs and the leather-bound book she gave to the stone giant.

"Those were Dearghs, right?" I asked him, just to be sure I wasn't making the wrong assumption in my account.

"Yes. Klibi's clan is about two hundred miles west of here. It's one of the ten active volcanoes left, though I'm not sure for how long it will stay that way."

"He called the woman a swamp witch. Is that the same species that sourced the succubi's illusion shield?"

"Indeed, Phoenix. Your vision must have been at least a couple of centuries ago, before the swamp witches vanished completely. You said she gave the Dearghs a book?" Draven asked.

"Yes. She said it held their knowledge and secrets and that it should only be given to someone who has the courage and strength to face Azazel."

"This is extremely valuable information. Thank you," he said, then lowered his head for a minute, deep in thought.

"Well, care to share?" Serena asked him, a tinge of sarcasm in her voice.

"It was thought to be just a rumor, but there was word that the swamp witches preserved their entire knowledge and spells in writing, hidden in three books that were lost throughout Eritopia. Now we know that the books exist and that the Dearghs of Klibi have one. There's enough power in those books to deal a serious blow to Azazel."

The Daughter rested her head on my shoulder, her arms around my waist. I welcomed her warmth and closed my eyes for a moment, quickly going over my second vision. A smirk made its way onto my face, and I let it take over.

"Oh, Draven, by the way, according to my second vision, your dad and Anjani's older sister had the hots for each other," I said, ending my statement with a light chuckle.

"What?" he hissed.

I pressed my lips together, smothering my laughter.

I looked over my shoulder and noticed Anjani by Vita's bedside, glaring at me as if I was Azazel himself. A shiver ran down my spine.

I described the entire vision to Draven. I told them about the passage stone that Almus had given to Hansa and their conversation regarding the swamp witches' books and further cemented my account by giving them full details of the kiss and the mention of introducing Hansa to Draven.

"Hansa never told me anything," I heard Anjani say, with disappointment in her voice.

"Neither did my father," Draven replied, clenching his jaw. "I never saw her here. I never met Hansa until the other day, which leads me to believe that this happened right before my father died. Before that full moon by which he'd promised he'd introduce us."

"I'm sorry, man," I said slowly, reminded of his loss and suddenly feeling like a bit of a jerk.

"That must be what Hansa referred to yesterday morning," the Druid concluded. "If my father and Hansa each had a swamp witches' book, then finding them is imperative. I'll need to speak to your sister again," he said to Anjani, then shifted his focus back on me. "What was the third vision about?"

I looked down at the Daughter, her temple pressed into my arm. Her violet eyes wandered around the basement, occasionally settling on me.

"I made it all the way back to what seemed like the very beginning of Eritopia," I answered. "I stood on top of Mount Agrith at dusk. There was a pool of water at the very top of the mountain, where its peak split in two. The eggs were never dropped on Agrith. They were pushed out by the water. They came from deep inside Eritopia," I explained.

"Did you see them?" the Daughter asked me.

Draven tilted his head.

"Yes," I told her. "I watched the eggs as they were pushed onto a ledge. They hatched, one by one, seven of them. They stood up, and they seemed to listen to everything around them, as if they understood the language of nature itself. They are deeply connected to Eritopia somehow. I know it in my heart, and I'm not sure how to explain that."

A moment passed before Draven shared his conclusion with us.

"If they were created by Eritopia, then they must suffer when Eritopia suffers. There must be some kind of primordial connection between the Daughters and this world. This could be useful to us in the long run, especially if Azazel continues to burn and destroy everything," he said. "I'm starting to think that the Daughters were a reaction to something, a particular event of that era. And the appearance of this last Daughter also seems auspicious. Just as Azazel's reign of death and terror begins to spread, Mounth Agrith gives birth to another Daughter. I can see the connection."

"I'm sorry I cannot be of more help," the Daughter mumbled, looking up at me. "I don't remember anything, and I don't know what I'm supposed to know."

I pulled her closer, my arm around her shoulders in a reassuring gesture.

"And speaking of strange connections, you and the Daughter seem to be linked," said the Druid.

"Wait, what? What do you mean?" I asked him, then looked at the Daughter.

"This is the second time I've seen something strange between the two of you. First, when she awakened from her shell. And now earlier, when you succumbed to the spiced rose mixture. As soon as you passed out, so did she. As soon as you woke up, so did she."

I blinked several times, trying to make sense of his statement. Serena looked at me and nodded.

"She fell flat on her face like a pancake." Jovi grinned.

The Daughter grumbled something in his direction.

Jovi's face dropped. "I'm sorry."

The Daughter and I looked at each other, as if trying to find that hidden connection. I felt equal parts torrid attraction and crippling fear, as usual. I wanted to hold her close to my body and taste her lips, but at the same time I was aware that she had the power to kill me, or anyone else, with a single touch. I didn't sense much else, and I felt too weak to attempt a mind-meld with her. I wasn't even sure it would work. Or if she'd allow it.

"Whatever is going on between the two of you, you both need to be aware of it and pay attention," Draven advised. "You could be connected in more ways than one."

I couldn't help but wonder what that meant. I felt myself sinking into the electrifying violet of her eyes. Was there really a connection of sorts? An invisible chord linking our bodies and souls? A string tying her heart to mine?

The latter felt like a probability, since my pulse raced every single time she looked at me. My body burned each time she smiled. My skin tickled wherever she touched me, sending billions of microscopic electrical currents through my muscles. We *were* bonded in more ways than one, and I had yet to ascertain whether that would be my salvation or my doom.

Vita

I wished it had only been a dream.

I slowly peeled my eyes open and sat up, my muscles gradually abandoning their relaxed state. Tension crept up through my back, stiffening inch after inch of flesh. I took a deep breath as I came fully into consciousness. One by one, the visions I'd had while I was sleeping started unraveling in my head, prompting me to search for Draven in the basement room.

Before I could call out to him, I looked down and saw black runes fluttering across my skin—hundreds of them in diagonal lines over my arms and chest. Heat expanded from my throat into my chest, and I screamed.

I was horrified by the prospect of becoming a full-fledged

Oracle—barren, blind, and covered in thousands of tattoos. The reality of my condition came crashing down on me at the sight of those symbols. I wasn't ready or willing to go through such changes.

I was swiftly wrapped in a pair of strong arms and held tightly as I struggled to scratch the runes off my skin. Bijarki's hands held my wrists, preventing me from harming myself in my fit of panic, while Anjani feverishly jotted down what symbols she saw on me.

"What's happening to me?!" I cried out.

"Take it easy, Vita." Bijarki's voice poured into my right ear, low and raspy, generating millions of tingly sensations in my spine. "They're fading away."

I held my breath as the runes gradually faded away. My eyes were glazed with hot tears, but my body relaxed in Bijarki's embrace. I resorted to counting my breaths to regain control of my senses, while comforting myself with the firm and muscular frame of the incubus enveloping me.

"You'll be fine," he said, as if only for me to hear. "The runes don't seem to be permanent. You'll be fine, Vita."

"But I'm turning, aren't I?" I asked, my voice trembling.

I looked up and found his silver eyes heavily shadowed by long, black eyelashes. His gaze softened as soon as it met mine, and I felt him take a deep breath before he let me go and took a step back. I knew he was being respectful and doing his best to keep his distance, but in this moment, I wished he wasn't.

"I tried to write down as many of them as I could," Anjani said, showing me the pieces of paper.

Draven and Serena moved from Phoenix's bed to mine. Serena took my hand in hers, and I leaned my head against her shoulder. Her presence soothed me while I combed through the memories of my visions in order to give the Druid an accurate account of what I had seen and heard.

I described the first scene to Draven, not skimping on any of the details of our capture. The memory of those glass spheres sent shivers down my spine, and I shuddered. I mentioned Azazel's words to the Nevertide Oracle, emphasizing his gratitude for her support. As if he would've never gotten to us if it hadn't been for her.

"This brings us back to our initial suspicions," concluded Draven after listening carefully. "It might not be Azazel manipulating the Nevertide Oracle's visions. She might be the one surrendering information to him."

"That's disheartening." I frowned and looked at Serena.

She gave me a weak smile, as if trying to reassure me that everything would be okay. But I wasn't convinced. I felt my mistrust toward the Oracle creeping through the back of my head, taking a firm hold over my judgment and amplifying my desire to protect my friends and my family from that dangerous lunatic.

"You have to take her current conditions into account, Vita," Draven said. "She's being held under water, confined to a glass bubble and who knows what else she's constantly being put through, either by Azazel directly or his Destroyers. He will stop at nothing to get what he wants, and we all know that torturing an Oracle isn't the first or the worst thing he's ever done to bring his nefarious plans to fruition."

I nodded slowly, then replayed the second vision in my mind first, wondering for a moment how Draven and Serena would react once I described it in full. I'd seen the look on her face. I'd heard his emotional confession. She meant more to him than he'd let anyone know. I did believe that she was already harboring feelings for the Druid in our present timeline, so I decided to keep certain details out and speak to her in private about their relationship, both present and future.

"The second vision was far worse," I said, clearing my throat. "I was in one of Azazel's chambers, the same black marble and rough limestone everywhere. He was holding Serena hostage, tied above a massive fire pit."

I watched Draven carefully, noticing the flare in his nostrils and the jump of a muscle in his jawline. If I didn't know any better, I would have said he was floored by my account. But the bandage over his eyes helped him conceal most of his distress, leaving me to interpret the tension in his facial muscles instead. Serena froze next to me, and I lifted my head from her shoulder. Her bluish green eyes were glassy, her gaze blank and lips thinned into a straight line.

"Serena was used as a bargaining chip by Azazel," I told the Druid. "You were brought in by Destroyers, Draven. You surrendered yourself in exchange for her life. Azazel even took pride in being a…Druid of his word, holding up his end of the bargain and tossing Serena away from the fire. She was still his prisoner, but at least she wasn't going to die. You sacrificed yourself for her."

A moment passed before Serena broke the silence, giving Draven a pained look.

"Why would you ever sacrifice yourself for me?" she asked him.

The Druid shrugged, unable or unwilling to offer an answer.

"From what I can tell, Azazel will find out about me and those whom I may be vulnerable around," he said instead. His head turned slowly toward Serena.

She looked down in response. Based on what I could see flickering in her eyes, Serena seemed conflicted and softened by the prospect that the Druid would sacrifice himself for her. I was willing to bet that the idea had already changed the dynamic between them.

"We clearly cannot hide from him forever," Draven continued. "We will have to be extra vigilant going forward. He cannot have any reason to suspect that either one of us can be swayed by using one of our own against us. It's how wars are lost and how people end up dying."

A frown drew Serena's brows together, and I heard her sigh.

But her reaction was feeble compared to the gasps and moans I drew out of the entire group when I described my third vision. As soon as I spoke about Draven dying and Azazel drawing raw power from his body and the many incubi and succubi left in the wasteland of Eritopia, everyone turned their attention on me, including the Daughter.

I told them about his exchange with Serena and his decision to invade Earth next out of psychopathic spite, just to get some kind of revenge against Serena, against all of us for opposing him and throwing wrenches into his wheels at every possible turn. No one said anything for a while. I couldn't blame them. I, too, had trouble coming to terms with the possible future. The horror was difficult to fathom.

I shuddered as I thought of my parents, grandparents, family, friends, and the rest of the creatures of Earth who would be faced with the wrath of Azazel if he made it to that point in the future. If he were to win.

"The Destroyers wield incredible power," Draven said, his voice soft as if treading slowly. He was most likely aware of what impact this vision had on me, on all of us. "I wouldn't be surprised if they did manage to escape from Eritopia at some point. We need to make sure that the Daughters don't end up changing their minds. It's the only way I see Azazel leaving this world."

"You think the Daughters would drop their defenses and let him spread out like a disease into other worlds?" Serena asked.

"Based on Vita's vision, it seems like they would. We will have to dig deeper into the future and figure out which events would lead to such an abandonment. After all, they do serve Eritopia."

"So, what do we do next?" I asked, no longer willing to sulk and worry about my Oracle transition or the nasty visions. The game had changed.

It was no longer just about Eritopia.

"You all need to rest for a while," Draven replied. "You've done incredible work, and we've made substantial progress. Afterward, we'll have to define a new plan and further investigate the string of events that will lead to that last vision of yours, Vita."

"Needless to say, the stakes have been upped," Serena added and straightened her back, pulling her shoulder blades closer together. "With Azazel potentially invading Earth, it's clear that we cannot, under any circumstances, allow him to destroy Eritopia. He must be stopped."

She spoke to all of us.

My gaze shifted from her to Aida, then Jovi, Phoenix, and Field. They all shared the same expression. Their resolve had changed. Concern no longer marred their features. Instead, I saw determination and a youthful viciousness I'd only seen during GASP trainings.

It took me another minute to realize that I was feeling the same way. Even if I were to go blind and whatever else the Oracle transformation brought down on me, I had a job to do. It was written in my genetic code, it was a part of my ethos. My family had spent generations protecting those who could not defend themselves, maintaining peace and unity between the most extraordinary of species.

There was no way we, their children, would be lesser beings than that.

I took a deep breath and took Serena's hand in mine. "I think it's time we start living up to the Novak name, don't you think?"

She gave me a self-assured smile, the kind that exuded the confidence and bravery we would all need on this mission.

"You're damn right," she said.

She didn't know it yet, but I had a feeling that Serena would soon be the force of unity between us all. She had the strength and determination needed to lead.

SERENA

We'd all shifted quickly from shock and dismay to solid determination.

Vita's vision of Azazel destroying Eritopia and preparing to invade Earth had gutted me, and judging by the looks on Phoenix, Vita, Field, Aida, and Jovi's faces, it had had the same effect on them.

We were made from the same cloth. We were raised to stand up and fight for what was right. And given how personal it had become, thanks to Azazel's future decision to invade our world, we seemed to have finally found our resolve. He had to be stopped, no matter what the cost was.

However, we still had a long way to go from acknowledging

these emotions to putting them into practice. Most importantly, there were plenty of unknowns still in the equation.

The last Daughter of Eritopia was with us, but we had no clue what she could do and how we could persuade her to stay by our side once her sisters claimed her. I knew, deep down, that the Daughters of Eritopia were of a single mind, in a way. Phoenix's vision of them on Mount Agrith had confirmed that suspicion already.

Our Daughter might be innocent and quiet now, but she might turn against us in the end. Or worse, she might leave us to be with her sisters and no longer interfere in Eritopian affairs.

The thought weighed heavily on my shoulders. I watched my brother's fingers fiddle with one of her reddish pink curls, lost in conversation with a creature who had the potential to wield godlike powers.

The one thing that gave me hope that the last scenario might not come true was Vita's third vision. I had a feeling that the Daughters could be persuaded to get involved if they believed in Azazel's potential destruction of the very world that gave birth to them. I figured they might decide to stand their ground, if persuaded early enough. I'd have to talk about this with Draven soon and go over options. I certainly wasn't ready to consider seeing the Daughters again, especially after what they had done to the Druid.

Our Oracles were slowly but surely coming into their own. However, time wasn't on our side, and the incubi's treachery had diminished our chances of a solid alliance against the Destroyers. We had to delve into the unknown and interact with creatures otherwise best left in the darkness just so we could gain some form of advantage in the battlefield.

I took a deep breath and closed my eyes for a brief moment. More and more factors began to pile up as potential obstacles. I'd have to go over them by myself, one by one, later tonight in absolute silence.

What really troubled me—and by troubled, I meant tore into me and ripped me apart—was the prospect of Draven dying. Every time my mind ran in that direction, my throat closed up, and my heart thumped agonizingly in my chest.

I shook my head and looked up from the dark green tiles on the floor, where I'd rested my gaze for a few minutes, to find Draven standing next to me, quiet and still. I suddenly felt the urge to hold him and revel in his firm presence just to remind myself of how real he was, of the mind-blowing effect he had on me. He'd become someone very important to me, and I wasn't ready to contemplate the idea of losing him.

"Anjani, Bijarki," he said.

Both joined us from the other side of Vita's bed, their expressions grave and opaque. I was aware that they had their own issues with Azazel, and I realized that everything they'd heard described by the Oracles had had a massive impact on them, on their own hopes for a better future in Eritopia. Their survival was at stake, as was ours.

"I'd like both of you to join me for a private conversation in my study," Draven told them. "We need to go over everything and recalculate some of our steps before going forward. Given these new visions, I think we'll have to make new preparations for this campaign."

Anjani and Bijarki nodded. I noticed the quick exchange of glances between the succubus and Jovi, who was still by Phoenix's side, along with the Daughter. Bijarki looked at Vita for a brief moment before taking Draven's arm and placing it on his shoulder to guide him out of the basement.

"I'm coming too," I said, unwilling to let Draven out of my sight or myself out of such an important conversation.

I moved to follow, but Draven turned his head, enough for me to see the side of his face while his broad back towered before me.

"It's all right, Serena," he replied. "You should spend some time with your friends and your brother. This conversation is between myself, Anjani, and Bijarki for now."

His tone was flat, something I hadn't heard since my first days at the mansion, long before I'd felt my heart flutter at the sound of my name on his lips and the feel of his body heat consuming me like wildfire.

I frowned but didn't say anything. I'd felt the line open between us since our first kiss back at the Red Tribe, but something had shifted again. A wall had risen between us, cold and quiet and unyielding. I felt nothing now, as if Draven had shut himself off entirely, once again pushing me away. There was a pang in my stomach and the fear of distance lurking in the back of my head.

I decided to let him have his discussion with Anjani and Bijarki first and talk to him later about this. I'd just started to open myself up, to allow new emotions to take over around him. I wasn't ready to let him slide back into his Druid shell. Not when I'd felt his lips on mine, his skin against mine, his soul pouring into mine during our mind-meld.

Instead, I turned my back on him and focused my attention on Vita. She seemed a little pale, but it didn't surprise me. She'd been unconscious for quite a while, and the visions she had experienced were haunting even from her description. I could only imagine what being in them and seeing and hearing everything must have been like.

"Are you okay?" I asked her, hearing Draven's footsteps disappear up the stairs.

Vita nodded and gave me a weak smile.

"We don't really know what we're doing, do we?" she asked, a tinge of dark humor in her voice.

"Would it give you any sort of comfort if I told you that I don't think Draven knows either?" I grinned, trying to keep my composure.

She chuckled and ran her fingers through her hair, resting her elbows on her slightly elevated knees.

"At least we're not on our own," Vita replied. "We're not alone."

"That we definitely aren't." I smiled. "Besides, you guys are making incredible progress on the whole Oracle thing. I feel so useless compared to you."

"Don't." A shadow passed over her face. "I still don't know how much of the Oracle gene is in us. Whether we'll go blind and whatnot. This was the first time I saw the runes on my body, and I don't know what to make of it. I have no idea whether they will become permanent, whether it will get worse. I don't know…and believe me, Serena, if you're feeling useless, at least be grateful you're not feeling the uncertainty that we're feeling, not knowing what we'll become."

I didn't have a reply. I hadn't thought about the impact the runes had on Vita's psyche. It made me wonder how Aida and Phoenix were faring from that perspective. If they were to go blind, I knew I would do everything in my power to help them, to make their lives easier.

"I'm sorry, Vita," I said, "but I won't let any of you fall into a pit of despair over this. Whatever happens, we'll get through it together. Draven's father was able to help Elissa, after all. Draven will do the same for you."

She looked up at me and pulled me into a hug. I held her tightly and felt her shudder in my arms. Vita may seem fierce sometimes, but she had moments when she needed reassurance that what lay ahead wasn't all death and gloom.

"I swear, I won't let anything happen to you. And whatever I cannot control, I'll do my damned best to make it easier for you. You are one of the most important people in my life. I don't know what I would do without you. And honestly, based on all this Oracle stuff, I'm pretty sure you'll end up saving our asses someday soon." I chuckled, and she laughed, her face nestled in my hair.

We parted, and she wiped the tears that had filled her eyes during our hug.

"I probably wouldn't be alive if it weren't for you, Serena," she said with a smile. "Which is why I have to be one hundred percent honest with you. There's something I didn't tell Draven about my visions."

I watched the corners of her mouth drop as she said that. Concern started chipping away at my demeanor. I counted my breaths in an attempt to prepare myself for whatever she had to say.

"What's that?" I asked, my voice but a whisper.

"When Draven traded his freedom for your safety, there were certain words between you. Like you had feelings for each other. You know…love," she replied.

"Oh," I blurted, not sure how to react.

It brought back the pain of Draven's potential death, and I wasn't ready to deal with that yet. My heart twisted in my chest, wondering why Draven would completely surrender himself to Azazel just to keep me alive. Why he'd give up this fight to keep me safe. I was a complete stranger, an otherworldly creature that he knew little to nothing about. Regardless of the attraction that surged between us, Eritopia was his world, the core of his existence, his reason to keep fighting.

"I don't know what to say, Vita," I mumbled. "It's a possible future, but I don't know what to tell you."

I did have an inkling, but Vita's mention of the word *love* sort of freaked me out. The attraction between Draven and me had become undeniable. It was a fact. I had made my peace with that and relished every second of it. But from that to Draven sacrificing himself for me—it seemed like a long road ahead, a product of time and factors I had yet to fully understand.

"I know. I'm aware of that," she replied. "But it has to start somewhere, right?"

I nodded.

"Do you two have feelings for each other, maybe?"

I sighed.

"There's definitely something going on between us," I finally answered. "I might as well admit that there has been a substantial shift in how Draven and I interact, so to speak."

"So to *speak?*"

Her left eyebrow was lifted, and her lips slightly pursed, as if telling me she wasn't buying the brief explanation I'd tried to give her.

"Well, neither of us expected this to happen," I said, feeling my cheeks flame. "We don't really know how to react to it, to each other even. So, we've taken it one step at a time, I guess."

"Just so you know, I'm pretty sure we've all noticed it."

"Noticed what?"

"That there's something brewing between you and Draven."

Leave it to Vita to put me at a loss for words as wave after wave of embarrassment hit me. Was it that obvious? Was *I* that obvious?

"Oh yeah, I saw it too," I heard Aida say as she walked up to us.

I hid my face in my palms, suddenly feeling like I was in a bad dream where I stood naked in front of a crowd of strangers. Aida grinned and nudged me with her elbow. I looked up and saw her winking at me.

"It's okay, Serena, I can't really blame you," she said. "The Druid is hot. Like midday in August hot."

I couldn't help but laugh, heat still sizzling beneath my skin. We all seemed to agree on that particular aspect, given the way we all nodded simultaneously.

"Well then, what about you and the incubus, huh, Vita?" I quipped, eager to shift the girls' focus away from me.

I had a lot to deal with regarding Draven, so I wasn't really ready to talk too much about him and about what had happened between us. Based on how he'd just rejected my company earlier, I didn't want to talk about something that had the potential to fizzle out with just one argument. The Druid and I were very good at arguing.

Lucky for me, Vita blushed all the way to the tips of her ears. I'd caught her with her guard down, and her expression confirmed my suspicions.

"There's not much to talk about," she replied, but I didn't want to let her off the hook so easily.

"No, no, there's definitely something to talk about!"

"Don't think we haven't seen the way Bijarki looks at you," Aida chimed in with a half-smile. "Although that probably is just his incubus nature."

"Okay, fine!" Vita conceded, raising her arms in a defensive gesture. "I've been having some trouble acknowledging it, but I think there's definitely some kind of attraction between us."

"Hah! I knew it! But is it real?" Aida asked. "I mean, does he affect you with his incubus whatever?"

Vita laughed, and I felt the mood lighten between us. So much had happened. We'd forgotten how to be just girls. We needed this.

"His incubus *whatever*?" Vita replied, still laughing, then took a deep breath. "He swears he's not using his nature on me, and I believe him. He's been nothing but honest and kind so far, so…I don't know."

"Did you kiss?" Aida grinned.

"Wow. How old are you? Twelve?" I smirked, and Aida nudged me again, this time with a little bit more strength.

We joked around for a while, teasing and questioning each other about the creatures that seemed to have taken hold of our emotions. Aida was coy when I asked her about Field, side-skirting my questions, but the glint in her eyes and the color that rose to her cheeks spoke more than words could.

For a few minutes, as we stood in the cold basement beneath a mansion protected by ancient magic, Vita, Aida, and I felt entitled to laugh everything off. Just for a few minutes.

Soon enough, the harsh reality would crawl back into focus and remind us of our possible fates. Soon enough, the thought of Draven dying would stab my heart over and over.

I quietly relied on Vita's visions of the future to help me save him. To help me keep him safe and fighting the good fight.

Every single creature in Eritopia needed him. Every blade of grass and every sunset. Even the last Daughter needed him. Most importantly, I needed Draven. He annoyed and enchanted me at the same time, and I was once again convinced that while I might get to experience sheer bliss if I lost myself in him, Draven might also end up being my undoing.

Jovi

I sat with Field and Phoenix on his bed for a while. None of us felt like moving around much, and the cool basement seemed to comfort us. We'd all heard Vita's vision of the future, and it had landed heavily on each of us.

My gaze wandered around the chamber before it settled on Aida with Vita and Serena engaged in conversation. Then I looked at the Daughter sitting on the floor, close to Phoenix's leg. She quietly looked over all the pages of scribbled charcoal runes. I wondered if she would be the one to save us or if she'd be the reason why the Daughters would eventually abandon Eritopia. I had so many questions that no one could answer. So many possible scenarios that could lead to that devastating outcome Vita had described.

I let a heavy sigh out of my chest, feeling a small amount of pressure leaving my back muscles along with it.

"I think you speak for all of us," Field said to me, the shadow of a smile passing over his face.

"Well, it's not looking all that great right now," I replied.

"You know what the worst part is?" Phoenix joined the conversation, while occasionally glancing down at the Daughter. "Before Azazel even gets to that point where he takes his Destroyers into our world, he will destroy Eritopia first if we don't stop him. I can't help thinking about the millions of creatures that will suffer and die *here* because of him. It just isn't right, man."

"Yeah, I feel the same way," I said slowly. "I mean, the succubi alone are extraordinary creatures. I don't know nearly enough about them, but what I do know is mind-blowing. I've only had a little time to spend with the Red Tribe, but they're something else."

"What's with that grin on your face?" Field asked, and I realized I was beaming like the Cheshire cat.

In my defense, I had just remembered Anjani pulling me into her tent that night after claiming me in front of her sisters. The way her skin glowed when she blushed heated me up from the inside. I wanted to feel that again.

"I was just remembering something from that night with the tribe," I said.

The guys and I hadn't caught up in a while. Not that we made a habit of discussing our feelings, but we had been raised together and were comfortable enough around each other to talk about stuff.

"I think I'm interested in Anjani," I continued and took a deep breath. "There's something about her that I've never come across before. She fascinates me."

"The succubi do seem extraordinary," Phoenix nodded in agreement. "But they're also genetically engineered to seduce, aren't they?"

"Yeah, good point," said Field. "Are you sure that what you're experiencing is real?"

"She keeps her nature suppressed around me," I replied. "She hates being a succubus because she wants genuine interest toward her, real affection, not nature-mandated drooling over her stunning body. I think it's one of the things I like about her the most."

"That and her *stunning* body," Field quipped, and I gave him a sideways glance meant to curb the imminent jokes.

"She was made to enslave and break men down, there's no doubt about it," I said. "But there's something more to her that interests me. Like a challenge of sorts. I want to find out all I can about her, but she keeps her guard up most of the time. She's not used to getting a man's attention, funny enough."

The silence that followed made me turn my head to find Field and Phoenix grinning at me like immature dweebs. I sighed, loudly enough for them to register my fake discomfort with their childish reaction.

"What?"

"You've got a crush, Jovi," Field announced.

"I'd do the Jovi-and-Anjani-sitting-in-a-tree thing, but I'm trying very hard to be an adult right now," added Phoenix.

"Yeah, I'm guessing you're trying to make a good impression in front of the ladies here," I shot back with a smirk. "Or shall I say one lady in particular?"

The look he gave me was priceless. His face turned red, and he quickly glanced down to check if the Daughter had heard us. She was deeply immersed in her reading of the runes, and I could almost see the relief wash over him.

"That was a hit below the belt, Jovi," he jokingly berated me, but I'd already been put on the defensive, and I wasn't done yet.

"You'll live. You're a big boy, after all," I replied, and then turned my sights on Field with the most serious expression I could muster. "What about you, Field?"

I'd seen him stealing glances at Aida during our little back-and-forth and decided to address that, since he'd been so eager to poke fun at me for talking about Anjani and the effect she had on me. He froze and looked at me, reminding me of a kid caught with his hand in the cookie jar.

"What about me?"

"What's up with you and my sister?" I asked, my tone heavy with a dash of warning.

Field blinked a couple of times, looked at Aida, then back at me. His face showed no emotion, but his irises flickered every time he saw her. He then shook his head, prompting a grin to bloom on my face.

"Nothing," he replied, his voice carrying a slightly higher pitch than usual.

"You're a terrible liar, you know that?" I shot back, close to bursting into laughter.

"No, I'm serious, I don't, I can't, I…" he paused and cleared his throat, trying to find his words. "I'm not interested in your sister, Jovi. I'm still…I'm still processing my breakup with Maura."

A moment passed before I replied. Not that I had nothing to say, but I was fond of Field, and I knew he deserved to be with someone extraordinary. And as protective as I usually was of my sister, it did seem like the right time for both to get out of their comfort zones and explore the possibility. I wasn't an idiot. I knew what those glances meant, even if they didn't.

"Hm, that's a shame," I said, looking at my sister. "In that case, you're definitely missing out."

"What?"

"Aida's an incredible woman. Any guy would be the luckiest creature in *all* the worlds to get her attention," I replied, perfectly aware of the blank look on Field's face. "I mean, she's been head over heels for you for as long as I can remember. It's a shame you don't see her like that."

I turned my head slowly to see his expression. I bit my cheek to stifle a smirk of sheer satisfaction.

Field looked stunned. He moved his gaze from me to Aida on the other side of the basement, and I could see his blue-green eyes flaring as she looked back at him. He immediately looked away, once again focused on my nonplussed self.

A minute passed. I could no longer hold it in, and neither could

Phoenix. We both laughed hard, further adding to Field's visible anguish.

"I can't believe you didn't know, Field," I continued. "You are blind. You've been blind for the past ten years if you haven't noticed something that we all knew. All of us."

"I mean, *I* knew. It was that obvious," Phoenix added with a chuckle.

Field looked at both Phoenix and me for a moment, then back at Aida. The girls were all the way across the room, and they'd only heard the laughter, not the context. Nevertheless, it was fun to watch the Hawk experiencing befuddlement.

He got off the bed, unable to take his eyes off my sister.

"I need to go. See you guys later," he said, without even looking at Phoenix and me, and hurried up the basement stairs.

I laughed, shaking my head. I watched my sister and her best friends for a little while.

I had a feeling that those three would withstand anything together—their bond was strong, and they somehow complemented each other perfectly. Vita was the introvert, but Eritopia had managed to bring out a side of her that none of us had previously seen. Serena was the firecracker, the curious and inquisitive one; and Aida was the fighter, the girl who always felt like she had something to prove— more to herself than anyone else.

I liked their dynamic and, given our current circumstances, I felt like they could really come into their own and accomplish some extraordinary feats together.

Field, Phoenix, and I had a different yet similar rapport—where one faltered, the others pushed until we reached our goals.

Occasionally, we helped each other out in more ways than one. In this case, I'd decided to snap Field out of his emotional limbo; he clearly felt something for Aida, even if he didn't know it yet, and there was no point in dragging it along without doing something about it.

Maybe it wouldn't work out, but if he didn't try he would hate himself for the rest of his life, and since Azazel and the destruction of everything we held dear loomed heavily above us, that life seemed shorter than ever.

"I can't believe he didn't see it," Phoenix said, amusement lighting him up.

"I know, right?"

Vita

Aida, Serena, and I went for lunch once I felt steady enough to stand up. The Daughter was kind enough to get the wards to change the menu a bit again. It felt good to diversify our food. It changed the atmosphere around the house in a way, breaking the routine.

I then left the girls to their own devices and went out into the garden. The sky was painted in soft pinks and vibrant oranges when I sat down beneath the magnolia tree, once again facing the dark green jungle beyond the protective shield.

The air was relatively dry, and a warm southern wind swept over the tall grass. Birds sang in the trees, their trills bringing me a sense of comfort. I had always loved nature and its sounds. My connection with it transcended the material. It was emotional, and the elements spoke to my soul in the bird songs and rustling leaves. It was a conversation in a language that I had yet to understand.

I placed three candles I'd brought with me on the grass—thick wax cylinders in clear mason jars. I needed the practice, and I'd realized that communing with the elements always brought me relief and comfort. I was in short supply of both since my visions.

The image of Eritopia reduced to ashes and dry stone, of Draven dying and Azazel laughing maniacally as he prepared to march into our world to pillage and burn everything down—it had all landed heavily in the pit of my stomach. My shoulders slumped, and my soul felt drained, as if hope slipped out of it, and I had no way of stopping the leak.

A few hours passed as the sun set beyond the jungle in lazy shades of red and purple. Darkness crept up on the world, but I was too busy playing with fire to notice anything. I had trouble concentrating, and I couldn't amplify the flames as much as I wanted to.

The thought of watching the people I loved as they died lingered in the back of my head, breaking my focus while I struggled to keep three flames burning high. I swayed them with different hand movements, but the fire didn't listen all the time, and I wound up frustrated when it flickered and died on its own.

I sighed and rubbed my face with my palms. The smell of wax was embedded in my skin.

The sound of footsteps in the grass made me turn my head. The

Daughter approached me slowly, her violet eyes curiously set on me. I smiled and patted the ground next to me.

"You can sit with me, if you like," I said gently.

I figured I could do with a little company, and her timid behavior reminded me of myself. In a way, she came across as a kindred spirit to me; she had enormous potential but didn't know how to tap into it. I had nowhere near her goddess powers, but I recognized the struggle and frustration that she dealt with.

The Daughter nodded and joined me on the grass, crossing her legs and tucking strands of reddish pink hair behind her ears. She looked at the candles, then at me.

"Playing with fire?" she asked.

"Trying, yes." I sighed.

"How do you do that?"

"Do what? Manipulate fire?"

She nodded. That was a good question, come to think of it. How *did* I control fire? How could I explain my entire being to this creature who had yet to fully comprehend who *she* was?

"Well, it's based on a connection. Something inside of me, a part of my being, is connected to the natural elements. My soul resonates with nature, and I guess we have established a conversation of sorts. The biggest challenge is to get the elements to talk back to me. I've been talking to *them* for years." I laughed lightly.

"So, you speak to nature, and it responds?"

She managed to summarize my fae abilities eloquently with one sentence.

"You could say that. I commune with the elements, I open myself up to the possibilities, and, if I concentrate enough, I can manipulate them and have them do my bidding. I am a fire fae, which makes fire my strong point, my life force in a way."

The Daughter nodded again, slowly, and looked out into the distance.

A moment passed before she spoke again. I watched her quietly, trying to figure out what was going through her head.

"And you're an Oracle, as well?"

"Yeah. I didn't know about that until recently." I shrugged, not sure how to explain something that I didn't understand very well myself.

"Phoenix is an Oracle too. And Aida," she said. "He told me an Oracle touched your mothers' bellies and that you were born and became Oracles, too."

"In a nutshell, yes. We didn't choose to be anything. It just happened."

"I understand that. I didn't choose to be me. You don't know who you really are. I don't know who I really am. But we both know who we are supposed to be, right?" Her question baffled me.

As quiet and clueless as she came across, the Daughter was able to present my condition—and hers—differently than how I had pictured it. She had a point. I knew what being an Oracle was about, because I had been told about it. It was the same for the fae side of me.

I wondered if it was time for me to stop listening to accounts of what I should be and focus more on being. The Daughter looked at me with a half-smile, and it felt like she could see right into my mind. A light flickered in her violet eyes as if she knew what I was thinking about.

"Think less. Feel more. Just be," she replied.

I hummed my approval and looked at my arms. My skin had become bronzed from the time I'd spent outside. I wondered if the runes I had seen earlier would return in a more permanent form every time I had a vision. The thought made me shudder.

"I know what the runes on your body said." The Daughter's statement pulled me out of my musings, and I turned my head and the upper half of my body to face her.

"You do?"

"Not all of it," she replied. "Some of the runes seem familiar, but I can't put my finger on them yet. Like the words are stuck in the back of my head, and I can't reach out to them. But I understood one phrase."

My pulse raced. I took a few deep breaths, mentally preparing myself for what she might say. Given the dark omens in my visions of the future, I didn't want to get my hopes up of the possibility that the runes could send a more positive message. My stomach churned.

The Daughter noticed my silence and cocked her head.

"When darkness swallows everything, it is up to the light to bring salvation upon us," she said.

I mulled over the words, trying to figure out what they meant. Was it a glimpse into the future like my visions, or was it a warning? Or a piece of advice from some superior deity sending its messages through our Oracle bodies, telling us that there was hope?

"I'm not sure I understand what that means," I ultimately replied, hearing the defeat in my voice.

"You are fire. Fire gives light."

Once again, the Daughter was conservative in her use of words yet infinitely more coherent than I could ever be.

"When darkness swallows everything," I repeated. "Given our circumstances, I believe the darkness is Azazel's doing, or Azazel himself. So, when darkness swallows everything, it is up to the light…" I trailed off, as the idea forming in my mind became clearer.

"To bring salvation upon us," the Daughter completed my sentence, never taking her eyes off me.

I knew what I had to do. If the runes were correct, then my inner fire could help against Azazel and the destruction he brought with him. I gave the Daughter a faint smile and turned my focus back on the candles.

Time wasn't on my side, and I had yet to get close to mastering my fire fae abilities. I took a few deep breaths, trying to empty my mind of everything that cluttered it, particularly my recent visions of death and the freaking apocalypse. But something kept holding me back. I felt it clutching my heart.

"You know, my mind sometimes wanders in different

directions," the Daughter's voice broke my failing attempt to concentrate. "It gets overwhelming because I don't know what is what, and I get dizzy and weak and frustrated with my own shortcomings. But then I think of Phoenix, and everything clears. All the pieces fall into place, and I can see where my mind needs to go. The many thoughts I have in my head unravel one at a time, and I can focus on something. Phoenix helps me think. Is there someone who helps you think like that?"

"You never cease to surprise me." Astonishment warmed me.

The Daughter was accurately tuned into everything, including myself and my thoughts it seemed. I figured she was in perfect unison with Eritopia as a default setting, given that she had been birthed by the world itself.

I was in touch with the natural elements—elements that were the same as back home. Fire, water, air, and earth. So, in a way, the Daughter and I shared some kind of common ground, which explained why she was able to understand me and identify the feelings that tumbled around in my chest.

Most importantly, she was right. The first time I had successfully communed with fire and manipulated the flame was when I had abandoned all thoughts except Bijarki. Even during breakfast that morning, my mind had run toward him as I developed that flaming sphere above the table. Bijarki was my catalyst, the only thought that helped me harness the fire within.

I put my palms out above the three mason jars and invited the image of Bijarki to take up residence in my head. The clearer he became, the quieter my other thoughts got, to the point where all distractions were washed away by the incubus who had been causing extraordinary chemical reactions in me.

I channeled my energy, using him as a cable of sorts, and pushed it outward onto the candles. Their wicks lit up on their own—yet another wonderful first! I gasped and moved my hands outward, beckoning the flames to follow my motions. One by one, the flickers grew and combined into one large sphere of pure fire.

I glanced at the Daughter quickly and noticed her wide eyes and silent enthusiasm. Overcome with gratitude toward her selfless support, I decided to show her something worth looking at.

I took a deep breath and allowed the idea of Bijarki to flow through my veins. I thought about his skin against mine, his silvery eyes drilling right into my soul, and the strength of his arms wrapped around my body.

The more I thought of each sensation that he had ignited in me that morning, the bigger the fire sphere grew. I stretched my arms out fully. I stood up and held the sphere in my hands. The flames licked my skin without burning it. It was as if Bijarki, even in his absence, was giving me the courage I needed to explore my unique relationship with fire.

I walked ahead with the incandescent sphere no longer connected to the candles. Heat coursed through my veins. It was delicious. The excitement fanned over the fire, and I raised my arms above my head as the ball swelled further outward until its diameter was bigger than the magnolia tree's crown.

I laughed and threw another glance at the Daughter. She stood up with a bright smile on her face and her hands clasped together, waiting to see what more I could do with my ability. I licked my lips and filled my lungs with air. Then, I clapped my hands once, and the fire ball burst into billions of sparks, bound together by some kind of gravity.

I turned around and moved my hands, mimicking a ballerina's pirouette, and the incandescent sparks flowed around me like ribbons of liquid fire, swaying with the wind and following my motions in perfect harmony. I could control fire through kinetics!

The happiness that rushed through me was impossible to describe. My heart was close to bursting out of my chest as I danced across the grass, followed by a wide stream of white sparks that burned as hot as my soul. I laughed, and the Daughter watched me revel in my newfound skill.

Aida

By nightfall, the more positive energy I'd accumulated from my conversations with Vita and Serena had slowly fizzled out, leaving room for doubts and the harrowing possibility of a full Oracle transformation.

I made my way into the banquet hall after everyone scattered around the house. I didn't feel very sociable, and I constantly checked myself for runes. I'd seen none since I'd awakened from my visions that morning, but I couldn't shake the thought of them returning permanently.

The warming plates were still out on the dinner table, and I was pleased to see the effects of the Daughter's intervention with the wards once more. I uncovered a hot dish and dipped my finger in it. *Delicious.*

I ate my dinner quietly. I'd changed into a pale green velvet skirt, settling for a soft ivory shirt with long sleeves and ample lace ruffles adorning the collar. I wanted to cover up as much of myself as possible, despite the high summer temperature. The less skin I could see, the smaller my temptation to give myself a once over for black runes.

As I chewed the last of my food, the double doors opened behind me. I looked over my shoulder to see Field walk in. The black trousers he wore hugged his muscular thighs, and his off-white shirt was unbuttoned halfway down with the sleeves rolled up, enough for me to see his broad chest and toned forearms. His long hair was tousled, and his left jaw was slightly red. Heat seared through my chest as my gaze lingered on his lips. I willed my gaze back to my empty plate.

He pulled out a chair next to me and sat down, leaning into his elbow on the table and purposefully facing me. I could feel his eyes on me, and all it did was further raise my body temperature. I replayed the morning I'd spent in his embrace in my mind, when I'd just woken up from the visions, still shuddering from the sight of my runes.

Neither of us said anything, until I finally gathered enough courage to look at him. His turquoise gaze was fixed on my face, but I couldn't read his expression. His eyebrows were slightly arched, though, enough to make me think that he was wondering about something.

"What's up?" I asked, my voice barely audible and higher than normal.

"Not much. Just had a sparring session with Jovi. It got rougher than usual, but it serves him right," Field replied with a satisfied smirk.

"Who won?"

"Who would you have wanted to win?"

His question confused me for a moment. I was unable to look away from those two blue-green pools of wonderful unknowns that made up a creature like Field.

"He does need to get some respect kicked back into him once in a while. I'll say that much," I quipped and took another sip from my water, grateful to have an excuse to look away before I lost control over my senses.

Field laughed and poured himself a glass.

"It will please you to hear that I wiped the floor clean with your brother, then."

I felt myself smiling but my heart wasn't really in it. I stared at my fingers on the glass, once again reminded of the runes. The persistence of my impending transformation was unbelievably frustrating, to the point where I realized I wasn't even able to laugh at my beloved brother's expense.

And Field noticed. "What's wrong, Aida?"

The sound of my name in his voice made me look at him once more. My body softened under his inquisitive gaze. My knees weakened, and my spine tingled.

"I…I can't get those runes out of my head. Every time I see them I'm reminded of my possible future, and it's not something I'm looking forward to. I don't want to go blind." I ended my brief rant with a heavy sigh.

Field held my gaze without saying anything. A dozen thoughts darted through my mind. I wondered what went on in his. His poker face was exquisite, and I found myself both loving and hating the mystery of it. Not knowing what he was thinking was a double-edged blade.

He broke the silence. "Do you trust me?"

There was a familiar twinkle in his eyes. He most likely had an idea. Back home, that usually meant upping the danger level on my GASP training with the addition of new weapons. I wasn't sure what it meant in Eritopia, but I trusted him with my life and soul and everything else I could give him.

I nodded, unable to utter another word.

He stood up and offered me his hand. I looked at it for a second and took it. His fingers gently folded over my hand, sending hot flashes through my core. He pulled me to my feet and tore off his right sleeve. My eyes went wide—both at the sudden gesture and the sight of his tanned skin stretching smoothly over his muscles.

He held the material up by both ends in front of me, and gave me a reassuring smile as he blindfolded me. I felt his breath tickle my cheek as he leaned in to tie the fabric behind my head. I felt hot and overwhelmed and tried to keep my breath steady.

Field took my hand again, while I got accustomed to the

darkness. The thought of going blind caused a numbing pain in my stomach, but I followed his musky scent and the sound of his footsteps as we went outside. I heard crickets chirping somewhere nearby and a subtle breeze above us.

He stopped, and I bumped into him. I forgot to use my brain properly with his body so close to mine. I held my head down, not sure what to say or do next.

"I need you to trust me, Aida," he said in a low voice that made my soul vibrate.

"I trust you," I whispered.

He wrapped his arms around my waist and pulled me close. I held my breath as I felt his body against mine, a perfect match of forms. He held me tight, and I lost myself for a moment. I heard his wings flap, and the ground disappeared from under my feet.

I squealed and locked my arms around his neck, holding on for dear life and gasping for air.

We were flying.

The air rushed against my skin, getting colder as we reached a higher altitude. The wind whistled in my ears. My core ignited, and my heart fluttered in my chest. I was soft against his firm body, and I relished every sensation.

"It's okay, Aida. I've got you," he whispered in my ear.

I felt as if I were in zero gravity, floating around as he flew with me in his arms. I held him tightly, my face nestled in the warm space between his neck and shoulder, struggling to control my breathing.

"You're safe." His voice seeped into my soul. His hands were firm and his grip unyielding.

I slowly relaxed against him. I learned to enjoy the weightlessness and the friction of cool air against my skin. It was delightful and scary and arousing at the same time. I felt my flesh melt into his and bit into my lower lip.

"I need you to understand something," he said as he kept flying. "Even if you lose your ability to see, I will do everything in my power to amplify every other sense you have. If you do go blind, I will help you fly. I will make you feel things that others can only dream of."

His words entered my soul and tugged at my heart, forcing a trembling sigh out of me.

I felt his fingers grasp the blindfold and pull it off.

I opened my eyes and found myself staring into two blazing turquoise gems. His beautiful face was framed by a giant pearly moon.

"Field," I managed to say his name.

I wanted to tell him something, to express myself. But my words had abandoned me. All I could do was look at him, his lips barely an inch from mine. He moved and flapped his wings twice as fast as we spiraled upward.

The cold began to sneak into my bones, and my muscles tensed. Before I knew it, I was shivering, but I didn't want any of this to stop. I clutched him and abandoned my defenses in his arms. I felt my lips part, and I watched as he licked his, his gaze softening and burning into my soul.

A concerned frown threw shadows over his face.

"Your lips are getting blue," he said slowly.

But I wasn't really listening. I wasn't feeling anything, other than my blood simmering in my veins. How could I be cold, when he had set me on fire?

I felt his hand travel slowly upward along my spine, his long fingers splayed and gently pressing into my muscles. The sky around us, riddled with myriads of stars, shifted as Field turned to descend. The air got warmer as we got closer to the jungle. He was all I could see.

My body glued to his, I instinctively pressed my hips forward to get even closer to him.

He tightened his grip on me, stifling a groan while his fingers dug into my flesh.

I could feel his rapid heartbeat echo in my chest.

The sound of wings flapping somewhere in the distance broke our stare. A hiss traveled through the night sky, and we both looked to our right.

We were just above the jungle trees when we spotted a flying group of Destroyers engaged in a tight turn as they headed in our direction. My heart stopped, and I held on as we dropped beneath the giant purple foliage. The obscurity of the jungle enveloped us as Field landed on one of the lower branches of a gnarly tree. Its crown was thick and dark enough to keep us hidden.

He leaned with his back against the trunk. My foot slipped. My legs were too soft for me to stand on my own. I gasped. He caught me before I fell and held me. I held my breath and closed my eyes, waiting for the dreaded sound of Destroyers flying overhead.

We were too far away for them to see us, I told myself.

My heart thumped in my chest. Field had a firm grip on my hips, while my palms rested on his rock hard chest. His lips pressed hot on my forehead. He said nothing as the Destroyers flapped their wings and hissed at each other while they passed above us.

We listened as they faded into the distance, thankful to have spotted them in time.

We looked at each other, finally able to breathe. Shadows moved around us, rustling the leaves just a few yards away.

"Destroyers are getting quite close to the mansion," Field whispered, then looked up. "Even with that protective shield, I'm not comfortable with that idea."

I nodded, unable to formulate a coherent thought. I'd been taken on an insane emotional rollercoaster, from the ground to the sky and back down to the jungle. I'd experienced excitement, exhilaration, desire, delight, and horror. We'd narrowly escaped a run-in with Destroyers. I was exhausted.

I leaned into Field. I rested my head against his chest and felt his arms wrap around me once more. I held on, and he flew us back to the mansion. The flap of his wings coaxing the wind to take us back to shelter soothed me.

SERENA

I woke up the next morning with a mix of anger and determination fueling me. Aida and Vita were still sleeping when I slipped into the shower and let the cold water wash over me, as if removing the last traces of doubt from my mind.

I needed to speak to Draven. He'd spent the whole of yesterday deliberately avoiding me after we heard Vita's visions of the future. I had to speak to him, to understand what we had to do next.

I put on a soft blue summer dress, a simple design with long sleeves. I wasn't sure where I'd find him at this early hour, but my True Sight brought me in front of his study door. I took a few deep breaths and walked in without bothering to knock.

Bijarki and Anjani stood by his chair, while Draven warmed

himself by the fire. It was blazing hot in there, and I began to regret my decision to wear proper clothes with sleeves. I could feel beads of sweat blooming on my forehead and down my spine.

They were talking when I came in but stopped as soon as they saw me—or heard me, in Draven's case.

"We need to talk," I said to Draven, my voice firm and sharp.

"Good morning to you, too, Serena." His politeness had a tinge of sarcasm in it.

I felt my blood boil. I glanced at Anjani and Bijarki. They both had a look of sympathy, but their lips were sealed. Anjani gave me a half-smile, and I nodded in return before focusing my attention on Draven.

"I need an update here," I replied. "It's my brother and friends that you're planning to use against Azazel, and I believe we all deserve to know what's going on."

"You don't need to be so irritable," Draven said, further infuriating me.

He had given me the cold shoulder all day yesterday, yet he was the one making it seem like I was overreacting.

The nerve of him.

"If you think I'm irritable now, wait until you continue to keep things from me," I shot back. "I need to know what you're planning. We all need to know what you're planning. You can't just shut yourself in here with Bijarki and Anjani and leave the rest of us out. That's not how it works!"

"It's not like you have any other choice now, do you?"

I leaned over to one side, enough to get a glimpse of his profile and the smirk on his face.

"Well, it's not like you can force the Oracles to tell you anything if you keep acting like an ass now, can you?" I held my ground, my hands balled into fists at my sides.

"Ah, good to see you're both back to your usual bickering selves," Bijarki interjected with a grin. "You were getting along a little too well for my taste."

I gave the incubus a look that spoke of a slow and painful death, and he put on an innocent expression and raised his hands in the air.

"So, updates?" I asked Draven.

He sighed, further adding to my irritation. As if I was the one being too annoying in this conversation!

"We haven't fully decided on all the details yet, but we know we have to get Sverik out of Azazel's dungeon," he finally answered. "We can use him as leverage to draw out the smaller rogue groups of incubi and succubi that are left. They need motivation to join our alliance, and Sverik's presence could help. He's very popular among his kind and has been known to influence the outcomes of several campaigns long before Azazel rose to power."

"Do you think he'd join us?" I asked.

"Given that we'd be the ones setting him free, he should. Besides, once he's out of the dungeon, Azazel will brand him a traitor, and he will have no other choice. With the Oracles, the Red Tribe, the Dearghs, the Lamias, and hopefully at least some of the

Sluaghs, we'd have enough of a solid base. Sverik would help supplement our forces. People tend to follow him."

"Yeah, I heard he's quite handsome," I snorted, remembering Aida's account of Kristos' brother.

Draven was quiet for a minute, and despite the dim light in the study, I could see a muscle flexing in his firm jaw. The fire threw playful shadows on his face and, for a moment, I forgot I was mad at him.

"Ultimately, with Sverik on our side, Arid will be compelled to turn his troops against Azazel's Destroyers when the time is right," Draven continued.

I nodded, processing the information while my eyes focused on his profile and particularly his lips. Heat bloomed in my stomach, and I inhaled deeply, willing myself back to a cool and controlled state.

"So, what's the plan, then? How do we get him out of the dungeon?" I asked.

"The trip there alone is potentially deadly. Too many eyes in the jungle, and too many miles between us and Azazel's castle to make it there without a Destroyer ambush," he replied. "From what we know now, the Dearghs travel through volcanoes, and there just so happens to be one still active a mile south of his castle. We need to explore this angle first and see if we can travel that way without being reduced to smoldering ashes."

"Why can't you flash us there like you did when you kidnapped us from the fae?"

He'd taken us from a different planet altogether using his magic, after all. What had changed?

"I can't do that anymore," Draven said, his tone warning me that he didn't wish to explain any further.

"Well, why not?"

Another sigh left him, and I grinned on the inside, pleased to see I was still able to annoy him. He deserved it for being so cold and distant and patronizing all of a sudden.

"The spell I used to get you all here cannot be reproduced so easily. It requires a certain powder that can no longer be found in Eritopia. It's ground from the bones of storm hounds, which are now extinct. I'd saved that last ounce for the possible scenario in which I'd have to rescue the Oracles from another planet," he explained.

The thought chilled me. It meant we'd have to find some other means of getting home… assuming we ever got to that point.

"What about the trip we took to see the Daughters?" I asked. "What spell was that?"

"It only works to find the Daughters," he replied. "I can't just zap myself from point A to point B whenever I please, Serena. If I could, do you think I'd still be here, struggling to find allies in this fight against Azazel?"

I pursed my lips and looked over at Bijarki. I opened my mouth to further engage Draven, but the incubus shook his head slowly.

My shoulders slumped in defeat.

"Bijarki," Draven called out to him.

"Yes, Draven?"

"I need you to go speak to Hansa about the Dearghs and the outcome of that conversation. You can use the passage stone, since you know where the other one is."

"Yes. But do we know if she's back yet?" Bijarki asked. "Based on Aida's account, she was still with the Dearghs yesterday."

"Chances are she will be back by sunset today," Anjani replied. "My sister never leaves the tribe for more than two days in a row. We're in day two now."

The incubus nodded and headed for the door.

"All right then. I'll be on my way now," he said and passed by me, giving me a sympathetic sideways glance.

I didn't like it. It looked too much like pity. I didn't need any of it. What was there for him to pity me for?

"Serena, you can leave us now," Draven said to me, his tone flat. "I have some business to discuss with Anjani in private."

I clenched my teeth, swallowing back a curse aimed at the Druid. I took a deep breath, gave Anjani a polite nod, and slammed the door behind me.

Anger bubbled up to the surface, burning through my throat and making my eyes sting. An upsetting pressure pushed down on my stomach as I made my way to the greenhouse. He was acting very differently, and it felt like all the progress I'd made in my rapport with him over the past few days had been thrown out the window.

The worst part was that he had completely shut himself off from me, and that hurt. I'd opened myself up to him, I'd overcome my own fears and doubts about him, and I'd allowed him to kiss me and touch me in ways that no one else had before. I felt like I had been tossed aside.

I looked around, my watery gaze passing over the multitude of colorful flowers and lush exotic plants. I leaned against a potted palm tree and started crying, unable to hold it in anymore. Hot tears streamed down my cheeks, and I wiped them away angrily, while more poured out of my eyes.

I felt rejected. Worst of all, I felt used. Like he'd gotten close to me for some specific end game that I knew nothing about. Like he was done with me and was back to his old condescending self. And I'd kissed him. I'd felt his fingers digging into my flesh. His hot breath over my face. His body hard against mine. His lips on mine.

I cried for a while, walking around as I let it all out. A lot had piled up inside of me since yesterday, but it had been severely amplified by his behavior this morning. I felt foolish.

It took me a while to calm down, but I eventually found my resolve.

I straightened my back and wiped the last of my tears away.

I didn't want to feel like this again. I didn't need that pain.

Most importantly, I was of no use to my brother and friends like this. I reached deep inside my soul for my determination. I found it and pulled it back to the surface. We had a dangerous road ahead of us, and I had to stay strong and focused.

Whatever had happened between Draven and me, as intimate

and as troubling as it was, it could wait. I pushed it back, willing it to disappear somewhere in a dark corner of my mind.

We had work to do.

PHOENIX

The Daughter and I went out into the garden after breakfast and walked up to the magnolia tree. The egg was still there, cracked open and dried up. She spent several minutes just staring at it, running her fingers along the sharp, darkened edges. It had been her home for many years, so I wasn't surprised to see her interested in it.

I sat under the tree facing the mansion. I was determined to do a little work on my Oracle abilities without the help of any herbs or potions. After Vita's visions of the future, I felt like I had to pitch in some more, dig deeper into the past. I wanted to provide the Druid with more information to help us gain a more significant advantage in the fight against Azazel.

There was no way in hell I would give that snake the opportunity to invade my home. It made me angry enough that he was destroying Eritopia.

As weird and as savage as Eritopia seemed, it was unique and had its own peculiar charm. Most importantly, the creatures who called it home did not deserve such a horrible fate. The whims of a power-thirsty Druid like Azazel could never justify these atrocities. And the closer I got to the Daughter, the stronger my urge became to protect her. It was her world, and I couldn't bear the thought of her suffering along with it.

Draven had told me several times that an Oracle could develop the ability to summon visions at will without any external help. According to him, it required a certain level of focus. I had to shut out any noise or image that could distract me.

I wasn't sure where to begin, but my goal was simple—tap into a vision of the past on my own. I leaned against the trunk and took a few deep breaths. I closed my eyes and sought out the silence. The noises around me began to fade away.

The bird trills faded, and the rustling leaves and the whispers of the southern wind gradually muted. It didn't seem difficult up to that point. However, I couldn't go beyond the darkness. It took me a while to accept that no vision would come to me with my eyes closed.

I tried focusing on something else instead. It was worth a shot. I set my sights on the Daughter, watching as she stood up and looked at me. The wind ran through her hair, lifting it gently in ribbons of hot pink with red reflections. Her violet eyes shimmered in the sun, and the smile she wore sent heatwaves through my chest.

She walked around, and I followed her bare feet in the tall grass, the white linen dress brushing against her thighs. As I took the whole sight of her in, I began to wonder what it was about her that had me so entranced. There was this invisible string tying my heart to hers, in a connection that transcended time and space. But I could never tell what she was thinking or feeling, no matter how much I tried. The mind-meld I attempted didn't work. She hadn't even felt my attempts to sneak into her mind, as if she were impervious to my sentry abilities. And yet I depended on her presence. Even more strange was the fact the she seemed to mirror my various states. If I was tired, she yawned; if I passed out, she passed out as well. I couldn't help but wonder how deep this connection really was.

She started picking wildflowers, putting together a colorful bouquet of purples and yellows, occasionally glancing at me. Each time my heart thudded.

I sighed and relaxed against the tree. Its bark dug into my back. After what felt like a quarter of an hour, my vision started to become blurry, but I didn't move. It was as if my mind was slowly detaching itself from the material world.

The view in front of me started to change. At first, it was so subtle I didn't even realize what was happening. It was as though a clear film had been lowered on top of the original image. There was the mansion, the tall grass and bright sun, the summery breeze blowing through the pink magnolia trees, and the wildflowers lazily stretching outward from rounded bushes.

But the Daughter wasn't the Daughter anymore. I recognized Elissa in her stead, walking toward the edge of the protective shield while picking flowers. She had her back to me, occasionally looking over her shoulder to give me a reassuring smile. Her dark hair was combed back in a loose bun, and I caught a glimpse of some of the black runes on her wrists. Her marks were permanent, but she didn't seem to mind. She had her eyesight and was grateful enough for that much.

My eyes burned, and my vision went blurry again, but I could still see her in the distance. I tried to shake off the uneasiness of watching her so close to the shield. With each step she took, my concern amplified.

Before I could say anything, she turned and blew a kiss in my direction. My cheeks felt warm. I didn't feel like I belonged in that picture.

Was that for me?

A slight movement to my right drew my attention. Almus, Draven's father, sat next to me, watching her. His gaze softened, and he smiled at her, pretending to catch the kiss she'd sent his way.

I was experiencing a vision of the past all by myself, with no herbal catalyst. I could feel myself beaming with pride as I turned my attention back to Elissa. My heart stopped once I saw her go past the protective shield, the invisible membrane glimmering slightly as she walked through it. I wanted to tell her it wasn't safe, but my words refused to come out.

The closer she got to the swamp, the more alarmed I got, to the point where I stood up and started walking toward her. The image before me trembled, and I saw Elissa fading away like a colorful mist.

I froze when I saw the Daughter standing outside the protective shield. She held the flowers to her chest and smiled at me. Shadows moved through the trees behind her, where the jungle began. My stomach tightened as the prospect of shape-shifters came crashing into me.

"Come back here!" I shouted after her, grateful to have my voice back.

Her smile faded, and she frowned at me, as if I'd upset her. She didn't know the danger that lurked behind her. I started rushing toward her, my heart thumping violently.

"It's not safe. Get back here now!"

The Daughter was still, watching as I ran to her. The confusion on her face only added to my aggravation. A clock ticked in the back of my head, as if counting down an unknown number of seconds before a shape-shifter would come out of the woods and attack her.

Not a second later, I saw one rushing from beneath a thick green shrub, ugly and livid and foaming at the mouth. It growled and jumped at her, its claws out as it slashed at her back. She screamed, and I stumbled to my knees, floored by a sharp pain in my back as if something had cut clean through my skin.

I watched helplessly as she fell forward, her flowers scattering all around. The shape-shifter morphed into her, hissing and circling her like a predator enjoying the sight of its weakened prey.

I reached around my back to identify the source of the searing pain, and I felt three long diagonal cuts through my shirt. My fingers ran over the wet fabric, and I pulled my hand back to find a worrying amount of blood smeared all over it.

It dawned on me that my connection to the Daughter was far stronger than I had originally assumed. My pulse raced as I struggled to stand. The pain in my back was so intense that it made it difficult for me to move without panting. I needed to get to her, and I was too weak to send out a barrier using my mental power. I tried to push one out, but barely a whiff emerged.

The beast jumped at the Daughter, going for the kill, and I shouted out in desperation.

An arrow whistled past my head. Its end was adorned with red and black feathers. It shot through the air and pierced the shape-shifter's neck mid-jump. The creature fell backward and writhed in pain, its shrill sending shivers down my spine and scaring the nearby birds away from the trees.

I then saw Anjani run past me, crossbow in her hand. She sprinted across the grass and reached the Daughter beyond the shield. She shot another arrow through the tormented beast, killing it. She helped the Daughter up and dragged her back inside the safe zone.

SERENA

Vita and I were in the basement, keeping ourselves busy with re-stocking the medicine cabinet. She'd read through some of the books in Draven's library and had learned to identify the plants and flowers in the greenhouse. Many of them had medicinal properties, and some had been used to treat wounds over the past few days, so the supply in the basement had dwindled. The herbs weren't something that the ancient wards were tasked with replenishing, from what I could tell.

I'd helped pick them from the greenhouse, and we were filling the carefully labeled jars downstairs when I noticed something slightly different about Vita. Her expression was stuck somewhere between pensive and pleased, a faint smile passing across her face occasionally. For someone who had seen the end of the world yesterday, I found that odd.

"What's up with you?" I asked, wrapping twine around a handful of twigs that looked a lot like rosemary.

Vita looked at me, her turquoise eyes wide and blinking faster than usual, as if she'd been caught red-handed doing something questionable.

"What do you mean?"

"You've been half-smiling the entire morning. What's up with that?"

"Oh," she nodded, while filling a jar with waxy dark blue leaves. "It's just that I had an interesting dream. I've been replaying it in my mind. That's all."

She gave me a weak smile and shifted her focus back on the jars, avoiding my gaze as if she didn't want me to drill any further.

Fair enough. She'd most likely dreamed about the incubus. Given how she felt about him, it wouldn't have surprised me. If anything, she deserved whatever she wanted—even if that meant Bijarki.

Speaking of whom…

"You know, Bijarki's going to see the Red Tribe again today," I told Vita.

She stilled and stared at me for a moment, visibly dismayed.

"What? Why?"

"Draven asked him to speak to Hansa about the Dearghs," I replied.

"I don't get why he has to send Bijarki over there. Why can't Anjani do it?"

She was visibly irritated, and I made a considerable effort to suppress my grin. I'd hit a sensitive spot, but I didn't regret it. She looked adorable when she was jealous. To be fair, I wouldn't have been comfortable with the idea of Draven surrounded by succubi either, especially after seeing them in the act of seduction.

I mentally shook the thought off. My stomach churned. I'd stashed him away in a dark place of my mind, and I didn't like him resurfacing so easily. I was still raw on the inside from his abrupt rejection.

"Anjani represents the Red Tribe in this group," I said, tying more twigs together before stuffing them into a spare mason jar in the cabinet. "She's been tasked to watch over the Oracles and, given the latest unexpected development, the Daughter as well. As part of the deal we made with Hansa, Anjani stays with us at all times."

Vita sighed and placed a jar full of pale green stems on the top shelf. She clearly wasn't okay with Bijarki on his own with the succubi, and I felt a bit sorry for her. I knew it had taken her a while to admit that she had feelings for the incubus in the first place, so not having him around must have been tough on her.

"He will be using the passage stone, though, so he won't be gone for long," I added in an attempt to comfort her. "Besides, I don't think he likes spending time around the succubi anyway."

"You think?"

I beamed at her, remembering our night with the tribe when I'd seen him constantly rejecting the succubi's advances.

"The night we feasted with the succubi and had that spiced rose drink they were all over the men in our group, especially Bijarki. And he kept telling them no, politely rejecting their advances, and keeping mostly to himself," I said. "I really don't think he's interested in them, if that's what you're worried about."

Vita blushed and turned away, mumbling something under her breath. I nearly laughed and wanted to ask her to repeat what she'd said, but a series of noises wafting down the basement stairs captured my attention.

In came Anjani with the Daughter, who had her arm around the succubus's neck and leaned against her with a pained expression. Phoenix came in after them, staggering and then leaning against one of the beds. He'd been hurt. Cold sweat seeped through my skin.

"What happened?!" I burst out and ran over to Phoenix.

He groaned as I helped him lie on his side. His shirt was soaked with blood. I ripped it open and gasped at the sight of three long cuts running diagonally from his right shoulder to his left hip.

"Oh, come on! Not again!" I snapped.

Vita helped Anjani put the Daughter in the bed next to Phoenix. She was in a lot of pain, crying as tears streamed down her cheeks. They put her on her side, and I could see the cuts on her back, through her ripped dress. They were identical to Phoenix's.

"Phoenix, what happened? Talk to me!" I said again.

Anjani brought over a bowl of water and a couple of towels. I nodded my thanks to her while she got back to treating the Daughter's wounds. My brother winced as I dabbed a wet towel against one of his cuts.

"She went past the protective shield," he finally answered, gritting his teeth while I continued to clean his wound.

Vita mixed a few herbs together, following Anjani's instructions, and brought me some in a small wooden bowl.

"Put it on his cuts. Follow the length," she said and rushed another bowl of the same to Anjani.

The Daughter hid her face in the pillow to stifle her whimpers.

"A shape-shifter attacked her," Phoenix added.

I wasn't done applying the herbs on his back when he sat back up.

"Hold still, Phoenix! I'm not done here!"

"You can do it later. I'm fine," he mumbled and got off the bed, as if entranced by the sound of the Daughter crying.

Anjani was busy covering her cuts with the same plant mixture.

Vita brought a few rolls of clean bandages from the medicine cabinet.

My brother leaned over and whispered something in the Daughter's ear. Whatever he said, it instantly calmed her down. The creases faded away from her forehead. He brushed a hand over her temple and caressed her cheek with his knuckles.

Anjani watched the exchange between them while her hands were busy treating the Daughter's wounds.

"There's something very strange going on between the Daughter and Phoenix," the succubus said.

"What, you mean besides the fact he's basically brainless when he hears her voice?" I replied sarcastically, frustrated with how vulnerable my brother seemed around the Daughter.

To most people, it might have seemed endearing, but to me it was cause for concern. After all, she was of the same cloth as the cruel goddesses who had blinded Draven and refused to help us against Azazel. We didn't know how much she really knew and what powers she held. I already had suspicions about the depth of this connection between Phoenix and the Daughter, and I wasn't eager to see them confirmed.

"Unfortunately, yes," Anjani replied.

I sighed, watching Phoenix whisper into the Daughter's ear, occasionally stopping to stroke her forehead again. She was in a lot of pain, but he seemed to be doing a very good job of comforting her. I waited patiently by the bed for the moment he'd remember that he, too, was in the same tremendous amount of pain.

"Remember yesterday when she fainted as soon as Phoenix went under?" Anjani jogged my memory, and I nodded in response. "Well, the cuts on your brother's back weren't caused by the shape-shifter that attacked the Daughter. They appeared on their own as soon as the shape-shifter slashed the Daughter's back. They were yards away from each other. I was right behind Phoenix. I heard him shout after her and decided to come out and make sure they were okay. I saw the blood spread across his back through his shirt.

He was on his own with nothing and no one close enough to touch him, let alone cut him like this."

She paused for a moment, applying the rest of the herb mixture. I watched my brother and the Daughter, utterly transfixed. Somewhere deep inside I had an inkling as to what was going on between them—I just didn't think it was possible, even though all the signs pointed to it.

"They are connected," I said.

Anjani stilled and looked at me.

I continued, "If one experiences something, so does the other. If one gets hurt, so does the other."

A few moments passed before the realization sank in properly. Vita was speechless, watching Phoenix and the Daughter with the same amazement. My brother heard us, but didn't reply immediately. He straightened his back and looked at Anjani, then at me, a frown pulling his eyebrows together.

"We're connected?" he asked, his voice low and raspy. "But…"

He seemed as baffled as I was. My heart stopped as one thought in particular started knocking around in my mind. After having recently been so close to losing my brother, it was a thought I wasn't ready to consider again.

"We already had some suspicion about this since the Daughter passed out at the same time as you did yesterday, but this confirms it. I believe your connection runs quite deep," Anjani replied. "Your reactions and your wounds are mirrored accurately. I'm starting to think that if one of you dies, so will the other—"

"Don't say that!" I immediately rejected the very idea that had been bothering me. "It can't be!"

Anjani sighed and nodded, an expression of pity softening her face.

"I'm sorry, Serena, but all signs point to that."

I took a deep breath, leaning into my fists as they sank into the mattress in front of me. We stood there for a while, watching each other.

"I had a vision outside, just before this happened, all on my own," Phoenix broke the silence, his eyes set on the Daughter. "I watched her picking flowers, then all of a sudden it wasn't her anymore, it was Elissa. I was reliving a scene with her and Draven's father, sitting next to me. Thing is, the Daughter didn't pass out this time, so I'm not sure how this connection really works…"

"Technically speaking, you didn't pass out today, you only had a vision, so there was no reason for her to pass out either," Anjani mused. "The other day, you were under the effect of some very potent herbs. It was your body that was affected and it's your body that's connected to her."

Phoenix nodded slowly, running his fingers through a flowing river of reddish pink hair.

The Daughter slowly relaxed under the effect of the healing herbs. The dynamic between Phoenix and the Daughter had taken a very dramatic turn, and I feared it could spell trouble for my brother, the kind I'd be unable to protect him from.

SERENA

I finished treating Phoenix's wounds once the Daughter relaxed under the effect of the healing mixture of herbs. Then I went looking for Draven. He had to know about this troubling development, and I needed to find out if he'd heard about such powerful connections before.

I found him in his study, warming up by the fire. The room was scorching hot, as usual. I instantly dripped sweat, and my lips dried up. Draven was in his chair, quiet and still, only slightly moving his head, enough for me to see his profile.

I got down to business. "There's a weird connection between Phoenix and the Daughter."

Several seconds went by before he nodded. "I suspected

something yesterday as you know, but it felt too early to tell. What happened?" he asked.

"If the Daughter gets cut, he gets cut. The Daughter went past the shield and was attacked by a rogue shape-shifter. Phoenix was yards away within the mansion's protective perimeter, nowhere near her at the time. The shifter cut her back, and an identical wound appeared on Phoenix's back simultaneously. Anjani got her back to safety, and we've already treated their wounds. They'll both be fine."

I told the story in one long breath. My nerves were frayed. Not only was my brother's life somehow linked to a Daughter of Eritopia, but my heart was helplessly thudding in my chest from standing just a couple of feet away from Draven.

"It might have something to do with Phoenix's sentry abilities," Draven mused, his index finger pressing against his lips. "He did spend some time with the Daughter in her shell. They most likely shared a profound bond in there, more complex than we'd originally thought."

"Have you seen that happen before with anyone?"

"No. This is definitely a first. They must have fused somehow on a deeper, primordial level. I'd never considered the possibility before the Daughter passed out yesterday along with Phoenix," Draven replied.

A minute passed in silence. I stood there, unable to move or utter another word. My mind raced in different directions, from Phoenix to the Daughter to Azazel and back, then to the Druid, the Oracles, and everything else in between. My brain felt like mush, and my legs refused to listen to me. I had every intention of leaving him there on his own, but my body did not compute.

"Thank you for sharing that information, Serena. I'd like to be left alone now," he added.

It was enough to make me snap.

"What is your problem?" I asked, blood simmering in my temples. "Why are you acting like such a jerk?"

"A jerk?"

It crossed my mind then that maybe he was unfamiliar with that term as an insult.

"Disagreeable," I replied with the first alternative that popped into my mind.

"I've been nothing but courteous," he replied coldly.

"Oh, really? You've been pushing me away and keeping this distance between us, and I don't understand why. What did I do, Draven? What makes me so unpleasant to be around?"

"You're mistaken. I just need to be left alone to think," Draven said.

But I wasn't buying it. "You're lying."

Silence stretched between us. I felt my pulse in my ears. Anger poured through my veins like liquid fire. And yet, all I wanted was to understand why he'd walled himself off like this.

"I'm not lying, Serena."

"You must think I'm an idiot. If you've decided to not be anywhere near me again, just say so. Stop pushing me away like

I'm a little girl. I think I deserve a little bit more respect than that."

"I can't risk *losing* you!" His voice thundered through the room.

He stood up to face me, his hands balled into fists at his sides. Tension flexed a muscle in his jaw. I'd finally hit a nerve.

My heart jumped into my throat, and I blinked several times, unable to fully process his words.

"What do you mean?"

He sighed and ran a hand through his hair.

"I've decided to put some distance between the two of us after Vita's vision of the future," he answered, his tone soft and low. "We are clearly drawn to each other, Serena, and I've yet to fully grasp the meaning of that or the ensuing consequences. But I do know that if nothing else happens between us going forward, Azazel will not be given the chance to come after you to get to me."

I didn't say anything. His words paralyzed me, and I waited to regain some kind of sense.

"I can't bear the thought of you getting hurt. And I can't lose this fight against Azazel either. Too much hangs in the balance. Eritopia, my world, and my life are at stake here." His voice shook.

His words tore me apart, but at the same time it gave me the energy I needed to respond.

"You're a coward," I replied, unwilling to let him off so easily.

He stilled, as if waiting for me to continue. So, I did—there was plenty more where that came from.

"If you do that, if you push me away, you're a coward. You're just giving in to Azazel, letting him win before we even stand up to fight him. You're conceding before you even throw the first punch. You are a coward, Draven."

I took a step forward, driven by an unseen force. The pain he'd caused me over the past few hours had been harnessed into a sense of determination that I'd been missing lately. I felt like I was unstoppable, and I had so much more to tell him.

"We are so much stronger together, but what would you know? You've been living in complete isolation since you were born. You can't possibly begin to comprehend the force behind a group like ours. We can't live in fear of one vision or another. We can't be afraid of whatever might or might not happen. We'd stop living altogether if we did! The Oracles don't have these visions for us to cower before the future, Draven. The Oracles warn us, so that we can *prevent* the future, so that we can work around it and make sure our choices take us somewhere good. If we stand apart because of one *possible* future, you might as well walk out of this mansion right now and surrender to Azazel."

The hot air filled my lungs in one deep breath. I'd said plenty, yet nowhere near enough. I didn't have the courage to tell him that I needed him close to me, that I couldn't see the future without him, no matter the outcome. But I hoped I had at least given him enough reasons to stop pushing me away like I was an undesirable stray cat.

Some time passed before I realized that he hadn't responded to anything I'd just said. He merely stood there, quiet. I started to worry, thinking I was about to get kicked out of his study for my impertinence. I may have been a little bit too abrupt, but he had been asking for it.

"Draven?"

Nothing. The silence weighed heavy, and after everything I'd just said, it was making me feel awkward.

"Draven, say something."

I watched his hand come up to his face. He removed the bandage from his head. I gasped as he opened his eyes, his beautiful gray eyes, and saw me for the first time in days. Sheer happiness washed over me, and in a moment of relief I totally forgot how mad I was.

The Daughters must have considered his debt repaid and restored his eyes.

Two whirlpools of stormy silver shadowed by long black eyelashes drilled into my very soul. I couldn't get enough, but I also had to remind myself of my dignity. He'd attempted to toss that out the window. Sight or no sight, he didn't deserve to get off that easily. I mentally chastised myself for softening up so quickly.

"Well then, it's good you have your eyesight back, so you can watch as I walk out of here. I don't work with cowards." I turned toward the door.

But before my fingers reached the doorknob, Draven crossed the room and caught my wrist, whisking me around. He wrapped his arms around me and crushed me against his firm chest. I froze, my breath stuck in my lungs and my body was tender against his.

His gaze softened, and his mouth took mine in a hungry kiss, devouring me. I caved in. My knees trembled, and my core ignited with white fire. I kissed him back, hard, parting my lips against his.

I felt his heart savagely beating in his chest, sending echoes through my ribcage. His breath faltered as we consumed each other. His hands traveled up and down my back as if trying to feel as much of me as he possibly could.

And then, just as suddenly, he stopped and pushed himself away, leaving me to struggle with standing on my own. I leaned my back against the door for a moment to get some stability back in my legs. My breathing was ragged and fast, matching the insane drumming of my heart.

He looked at me, fires burning in his eyes. His lips were red and tender, and his chest moved with deep inhalation. His face took on a pained expression that rang alarm bells in my head.

"I'm sorry, Serena. I am so sorry," he sighed.

I waited for him to continue. I was too numb to say anything. I was too hot and too vulnerable to even consider a negative outcome from this conversation.

"I can't… I am too…vulnerable around you, Serena. You're… You'll be the end of me if I don't put a stop to this now. I gave in to my instincts. I was so happy to see…to see you again. I'm sorry."

My stomach dropped like a stone. My heart followed suit, but I forced myself to maintain a dignified position and turned the pain of his rejection into furious energy.

I left, slamming the door behind me. I couldn't be in the same room with him anymore. My heart was stung. Tears welled in my eyes.

I sought the comfort of the greenhouse once more. I couldn't stand being pushed and pulled like this. My feelings were hurt. My pride was torn. I'd only wanted to be close to him, and he'd given me one more taste of his heaven before shutting me out again.

Cruel and heartless jerk.

Vita

I was becoming desensitized to seeing my friends injured. Phoenix in particular had made a habit of getting himself patched up almost once a day. The shock and grief had become part of my daily existence, and I realized that I'd learned to set my emotions aside and focus on the healing. I was good at nursing someone back to health, especially now that I knew the purpose of each herb in the medicine cabinet.

I left the basement with a frown but no longer distraught by Phoenix's or the Daughter's injuries. They'd been treated and were resting, and Anjani watched over them.

I was worried about Phoenix and his connection to the Daughter, but I shook the thought away. It was too early in the day to bring myself down with such gloom. It had taken me a while to get over my visions from yesterday, and I was too tired emotionally to deal with another potentially grim outcome.

After all, I had a surprisingly good dream keeping me company from the previous night. It had involved Bijarki holding me, whispering sweet words into my ear, words I could no longer remember. But his touch and his raspy voice had lingered well into the early hours of the morning, when I woke to a bright sunrise beaming through my window.

The dream tempered my fears, pushing me to smile and giving me enough energy to face my visions of the future and tell them, "Not on my watch!" It seemed like no matter where I was, whether in a dream or in reality, Bijarki's presence had a positive effect on me. He made me feel strong enough to fight.

I reached the bottom of the stairs leading to the upper floor of the mansion. The temperature had risen by several degrees, making it necessary for me to change out of a dark green velvet dress into something lighter. I remembered there was a soft linen dress on a chair in our room.

I nearly bumped into Bijarki as he came downstairs. I froze, my foot on the first step, and he stilled, his body so close to mine. I had to crane my neck back a little to see him. His deep eyes studied mine. I noticed the duffel bag on his shoulder and raised my eyebrows.

"I'm going to visit the Red Tribe," he said. His expression was difficult to read.

I already knew where he was going, but I had yet to find a way to hide my displeasure. Given how honest he'd been with me the day before, I decided that he deserved the same from me.

"I heard, but I can't help but worry," I replied, my voice barely a whisper.

"I'm a big boy. I can handle myself around a few succubi." His gaze softened, and he gave me a boyish smile.

His attempt to reassure me made my heart flutter, but I still wasn't comfortable with him going away. It made me anxious.

"I'd like to come with you," I said, surprised by my own request.

He took a deep breath, quietly scanning me from head to toe.

"As much as I would love to take you with me, Vita, it is much too dangerous for you. Azazel sensed your presence from the moment you entered Eritopia. As soon as you leave the protection of the mansion's shield, you will be vulnerable. Azazel will know and will eventually trace you back here."

I sighed and nodded in agreement, but my heart felt heavy nonetheless. "You're right. It was a dumb suggestion. It's just that I've been stuck here for quite some time now, and I can't help but feel trapped in this place. It's frustrating."

He walked forward slowly.

I stepped back.

He reached the bottom of the stairs. He stopped with an inch between us. I felt his hot breath over my face, setting my body ablaze from the inside. His lips parted and stretched into a seductive smile that stirred me.

"I'm sorry to hear you're having such a tough time here, Vita. I'd be happy to make it more enjoyable for you. But you'll have to wait until I get back."

His voice sent shivers down my spine and dried my mouth. I licked my lips. The air was suddenly very hot and dry around me, and my breath came in uneven gasps. My cheeks flamed.

I couldn't move. Whatever he was doing, it had a paralyzing effect on me.

"Are you using your incubus abilities on me right now?" I whispered.

He shook his head, devouring me with his silvery gaze.

"Whatever you might be feeling right now, Vita, I assure you it's yours and yours alone," he said, then leaned in close enough to whisper in my ear. His lips brushed against my lobe. "I told you I'm doing my best to keep my nature under control when I'm around you, and that hasn't changed. I wouldn't want to sway you in any way, little fae. But I do find this delightful, watching you blush every time our eyes meet. I'm already looking forward to my return."

His words poured right into my soul, and I found myself defenseless before him.

He dropped a soft kiss on my cheek.

I closed my eyes, overwhelmed by the delicious sensation of his lips against my skin. I held my breath, afraid to let it go and lose the moment altogether.

I didn't realize when he straightened his back and put some

distance between us. When I opened my eyes, I found him looking at me. His gaze dropped on my lips. His pupils dilated and nostrils flared.

"I'll be back soon. I promise," he said. He bowed politely and left me there.

I was speechless, and my knees threatened to give in. I leaned against the solid wood railing, trying to catch my breath. A smile sliced my face from left to right, and my very core hummed from the memory of his husky voice whispering in my ear.

Soon didn't seem like soon enough.

AIDA

I'd woken up that morning with a strong sense of determination. I'd gone to bed torn between the fear of the darkness Vita described in her vision, and the arousing experience I'd had during my flight with Field.

A single thought persisted in my mind. As Oracles, we had the ability to see through time. We had the power to prevent what we saw in the future, learn from the past, and draw valuable intel from the present.

I had a valuable part to play in this.

My knowledge of the present could help shape our decisions, informing us of what went on throughout Eritopia and giving us a better advantage against Azazel.

I took a cold shower and slipped into a pair of beige trousers and one of the shirts left in our room. Then I rushed downstairs for some hot, soul-healing coffee.

Two cups later, I climbed the stairs to the attic.

I opened the windows wide enough to let the fresh air in. I crossed my legs in a meditation pose and spent some time in silence, breathing in and out in a controlled rhythm.

I knew what I had to do.

I needed to tap into my visions of the present without any herbal or physical aids. I was an Oracle, damn it, and I had to learn to be a good one fast. The Druid had talked about focusing and clearing our minds to achieve the mental state needed to tap into our visions, so I figured I'd try a little Zen and work my way up from there.

It took me a while to fully block out all the background noise— the birds chirping outside, the wind rustling through the tree crowns, my own heartbeat.

I wasn't sure when the transition happened, but I found myself standing in the middle of a dark jungle, somewhere in Eritopia where the sun couldn't pierce through the thick foliage. Murky water snaked alongside the narrow path ahead of me, and shadows moved between the gnarly trees.

Three succubi walked through me from behind, as if I were made of mist. They couldn't see me, as usual, but I could see and hear them. They were young and strong, clad in black leather, and proudly displaying their red war paint and the scarlet feathers braided in their charcoal manes. Wide swords hung heavily from their belts. They walked to the end of the path, where a mountain stood tall and a cave opened at its base.

The one on the left carried a dead body wrapped in animal hides and tied with leather strings on her shoulder. Silver blood dripped from one end, leaving a trail behind them.

I didn't like the feel of this scene. It was too dark and riddled with whispers and an overall feeling of something terrible about to happen. And the corpse... I shuddered.

Nevertheless, I followed them into the cave. None of them said anything as they went deeper into the mountain. The path was lit by small torches mounted on the cave walls.

Their white knuckled hands gripped the hilts of their swords. The succubi didn't seem comfortable, but they didn't back down.

We reached a wide circular chamber, with a channel dug all around the wall that was filled with dark water. Several creatures sat in the middle, feeding off the corpse of a large long-tusked animal that resembled a pachyderm.

The feeding creatures seemed familiar. One by one, they sniffed the damp air and caught the scent of their visitors. They stood.

I gasped at the sight of them. They looked like incubi and succubi, but there was something horribly off about them. Their bodies were thin with white flaky skin, black eyes, and dark, rotten teeth bared in hissing grins.

The succubus in the middle addressed these gruesome creatures first, visibly disgusted by their jaws smeared with animal blood.

"We're here to speak to Krol," she declared, her tone heavy and determined.

Two of the creatures approached the succubi, but the scraping of swords being pulled out of their sheaths stopped them in their tracks. They took a few steps back, weary of retaliation. They hissed at each other, as if communicating. I held back a gag. They were so creepy.

The water in the canal splashed against the stone wall as something slithered beneath its surface. There was a creature in there.

The succubus on the left dumped the heavy load she'd been carrying on the floor, using the sword to cut off the leather strings and reveal the corpse inside.

I walked closer.

It was an incubus. He had been stabbed several times in the chest, judging by his wounds.

"Come out here, Krol!" the succubus in the middle shouted, her voice echoing around the cave. "We heard you needed a body. Got you a fresh one, right here!"

Before I could blink, a large, gray worm crawled out of the dirty canal water. It reminded me of a tapeworm, its mouth circular and riddled with razor-sharp teeth. It slithered across the cave floor, passing the other creatures and the dead animal, and stopped next to the deceased incubus.

It pushed its head into the corpse's mouth and wiggled until it vanished inside.

"Oh ugh, ugh, ugh!" I exclaimed, utterly disgusted and thankful that no one could hear me. "That is just so wrong!"

I stilled and swallowed my words when the dead incubus opened its eyes. Its pupils were black as it sat up and looked around with a blank expression. I then made the connection. The creatures feeding on the dead animal—they looked like incubi and succubi because they *were* incubi and succubi. Their dead bodies were animated by these parasitic worms. I shuddered.

"There you go, Krol. A nice new body for you to enjoy," the succubus in the middle said.

"Thank you, distinguished general," the creature replied with a ragged breath, as if still adjusting to the new meat suit. "I assume you want something in return, other than to walk out of here with your beautiful bodies intact?"

"We want you to meet with Hansa of the Red Tribe and discuss an alliance against Azazel. He's getting stronger, and people are dying, including your Sluaghs," she replied. She kept her chin up, but she couldn't quite mask her disgust.

The vision before me faded, and I cursed at my inability to hold it steady for long enough to gather more information. But as the darkness of the cave cleared out and I felt the warm attic light wash over me, I took a deep breath and felt thankful to still be here and not stuck in that cave.

So those are Sluaghs.

I shuddered again.

I did it.

The joy that came over me was delightful. I'd had a vision all by myself, without any external influence. I stilled. I noticed the black runes dancing across my skin again. I took a deep breath and let out an exasperated groan, as the markings disappeared one after the other. Soon enough, my skin was clear again.

It seemed like a recurring phenomenon that synchronized with the visions. Fortunately, for now, they weren't permanent. I stifled the glimmer of hope that perhaps they would never be permanent in an attempt to prepare myself for the worst.

I ran downstairs, eager to get a hold of the Druid and tell him what I had accomplished and what I had seen. I looked around the ground floor and made my way into the banquet hall. Vita and Serena were grabbing lunch. The rest of the house seemed particularly quiet.

"Where's everybody else?" I asked. A grin slit across my face at the sight of food.

The growl in my stomach reminded me that I hadn't eaten and that I was positively ravenous.

"Somewhere in and around the house," Vita replied. "Bijarki's away. Field's probably out flying."

I sat down and helped myself to a full plate of food from the warming dishes. I tucked in, thinking I'd find the Druid after I finished my meal and tempered my loud stomach.

"What's wrong with you two?" I asked, noticing their sullen moods.

"Nothing. Just tired." Serena glared at her plate and stabbed a potato with her fork.

I didn't persist. I figured I'd ask them both again later. Whatever they were going through, it was obviously still fresh.

Vita looked sad and dreamy at the same time. I figured it must've had something to do with Bijarki. Serena, on the other hand, was a bundle of raw nerves, and I wondered what was causing her so much pain, but I knew she would open up when she couldn't hold it in anymore.

"I had another vision," I said, changing the subject.

They both looked up at me, their faces lit with surprise.

"I had a vision on my own, to be precise. No intervention, no weird plants, nothing like that. I sat down, I tuned everything out, and I channeled myself into a vision of the present." I beamed with pride.

"That's amazing, Aida!" Serena smiled. "Amazing progress."

"Yup, it is." I nodded. "I saw three succubi meeting with the Sluaghs, but I couldn't find out much more, other than a name. I'm not yet in full control of these visions, but I have to tell you, I saw enough of those Sluaghs to last me a lifetime already!"

"What do they look like? I'm having a hard time picturing them," Serena said.

"They basically look like giant tapeworms," I replied with a shudder. "They slither into incubi corpses and animate them like the grossest puppet masters I have ever seen. They're weird. That's all I'll say. I'm just sorry I couldn't see more this time."

"You'll get there," said Vita, even as she looked unnerved by my description. "As will I, for that matter. We've made it this far, right?"

"We totally have." I grinned. "Where's the Druid?"

Serena's face dropped at my question. I realized that whatever was bothering her was clearly related to him.

"I need to tell him what I saw," I added.

"I don't know, and I don't care," Serena replied, chewing furiously. "He can rot in hell as far as I'm concerned."

"Whoa," I raised my hands in a defensive gesture, surprised by her anger. "What did he do to make you this mad?"

Serena sighed and leaned against the back of her chair, a look of defeat drawing her eyebrows closer together. "He's a jackass. That's all. An absolute jackass."

Jovi

A day had passed since Aida's unaided vision, and a few days had passed since we'd returned from our trip up north to the Red Tribe. I hadn't seen much of Anjani. She spent most of her time deliberately keeping her distance from me—keeping an eye out for the Daughter, or gathering her special herbs and roots from the woods nearby.

I was getting frustrated. I wanted to see more of her, and I had made it my mission to learn more about her kind just to get an upper hand in this unexpected dynamic between us. I'd read up on some of the books about the incubi and succubi in the Druid's library just to kill time in between training sessions with Field, Aida, and Phoenix.

I'd come across a few interesting nuggets while studying the biology of the succubi. Their emotions were expressed through light cells embedded in their skin, which was why the succubi glowed when highly aroused or when they blushed. While in our case, the blood rushed through and reddened our cheeks as a reaction to certain events, the succubi's light cells—the same cells responsible for that beautiful silvery shimmer—were activated. I found the process to be very interesting and decided that I wanted to see it again on Anjani.

That morning, I went looking for her. I checked the banquet hall, the gardens, and the study and ultimately found her in the greenhouse. She'd slipped back into her tribal leathers. My lower body seemed delighted by that decision. She was cutting some strange looking flowers with bright yellow petals from their stems and carefully placing them on a piece of dry cloth on the ground. They looked like snapdragons, but the petals' edges were black.

I watched for a while as her fingers grasped each stem without touching the petals. She used a pair of small shears to remove them from the stems planted in a large clay pot. She crouched to better see what she was doing.

"Is it just me or are you trying not to touch the petals?" I asked.

She gasped and immediately withdrew her hands from the pot as if avoiding a flame. She cursed under her breath, then shot a death glare my way. Her gold and emerald eyes glinted angrily.

"You could've killed me!"

"Sorry I startled you, but how could I have killed you?" I asked.

"Is gardening in Eritopia lethal?"

Anjani took a deep breath and stood up with her eyes closed, as if mustering all the patience she could find. Judging by the way her nostrils flared, she didn't have that much.

"These are not ordinary flowers. They're extremely rare and extremely poisonous," she explained. "The toxin is deadly and spread throughout each petal. A single touch can kill me in under a minute."

"Oh, I'm sorry," I replied, mentally chastising myself. "Why aren't you wearing any gloves, if they're so toxic?"

"I am a succubus. I do not fear death. I dance around it. Gloves are for weaklings. I was raised to collect poison."

I nodded, processing that information. An awkward silence ensued. We stared at each other. I felt bad for my ignorance of Eritopian flora and had no idea what to say next. The prospect of her dying from that flower still blared in my head.

"Just try to make yourself heard before you walk into the greenhouse next time, that's all. Just in case I'm doing something like this again," Anjani conceded. "You couldn't have known, anyway."

Relief washed over me, reminding me of just how easily my emotions were manipulated by the succubus. I had never felt so vulnerable before, and I wasn't sure how to handle it. I'd been raised to be strong and fierce, and she seemed to effortlessly break me down without even trying that hard.

"What are you doing with those flowers anyway? Although I

must say, the term 'flower' is far too pretty for how deadly these things are," I quipped, hoping to relieve some of the tension.

She collected the poisonous blossoms in the cloth and pushed the flower pot back under the large iron table where it belonged.

"The flowers are called Death's Kiss," Anjani explained. "Their poison is the only thing known to expel a Sluagh out of its host and instantly kill it."

I'd heard about the Sluaghs, but I didn't have enough knowledge about them to fully understand what she was talking about. She looked at me and most likely noticed my blank expression.

"Aida described her most recent vision involving a meeting between Sluaghs and some of my sisters. They are deceitful creatures, filthy parasites feeding off the dead bodies of my kind. I cannot bring myself to trust them. So, I'm preparing for the worst-case scenario in which I may have to kill as many of these worms as possible," she added.

"What are the Sluaghs, exactly? I didn't get too many details from my sister yesterday."

"Sluaghs are parasites, basically. They live in the swamp waters and look like overgrown worms. They are extremely vulnerable in their true form, hence why they take over dead bodies of incubi and succubi. They animate the corpses like puppet masters and feed off them," Anjani elaborated. "A mature Sluagh can occupy a dead body for a long time before the flesh dries up and the host becomes uninhabitable. It's a strange process that we have yet to fully understand, but the Sluaghs have evolved to this point over millennia. For a long time, we didn't even know they existed. We feared our walking dead instead."

She placed the cloth bundle on the table and started cutting the red leaves off a small rounded bush in another pot. One by one, she placed them inside a mason jar, which she labeled.

"Your walking dead?" I asked.

"Well, yes. A long time ago, back when the world was still young, we buried our dead out by the river. We believed that the water fed the ground and that our dead helped nourish it further, giving life to flowers and trees. In some parts, the Sluaghs ran through the rivers. They would often dig into the bank and find the bodies. The next day, our villages were attacked by our dead relatives, walking and hissing and hungry for our flesh."

I let out a sigh, picturing one such village and the horrible scene that Anjani had just described. This had once been a regular part of Eritopians' lives. It gave me chills.

"It just so happened, a thousand or so years ago, that there was a succubi tribe living on the southern slope of Mount Agrith, where Death's Kiss flowers grow in abundance. They had just settled there, after having been driven out of an incubus citadel. One of the two waterfalls of Agrith poured into a river we call Sol, and its waters were infested with Sluaghs, but the succubi didn't know that yet.

"Soon enough, they lost a few sisters to a pack of shape-shifters and recovered the bodies. They buried them in the bank, as usual.

The dead sisters came back at night, with black eyes and rotten teeth, demanding the flesh of the living. The wind was strong, and it blew over the Death's Kiss bushes bordering the camp. Some petals flew off and got stuck on the Sluaghs' new bodies. The poison instantly entered the flesh and expelled the worms. They died a most agonizing death, and the bodies of the sisters were once again still and lifeless. It was then that we learned about the Sluaghs' true form and what they really were." She put a lid on the jar. "Soon after, we began to study them and their ways. They can hold on to a body for years, cheating their way through unnaturally long lives."

Some time passed before either of us said anything. I watched her quietly as she collected more herbs from various pots in the greenhouse.

"Why have you been avoiding me?" I asked, determined to address the elephant in the room.

She stilled and looked at me, eyes wide and genuinely surprised.

"I…I haven't been avoiding you," she stuttered. "I've been…I've been busy."

"Yeah, busy avoiding me."

I took several steps toward her, closing the distance between us. I wasn't sure where my courage came from. She tilted her head back to look me in the eyes. I could hear her heart beating faster, echoing in my ears.

"No, I… Not everything I do revolves around you, wolf-boy," she replied, looking away and blinking fast.

Gold and emerald flakes flickered in her eyes, and I could see her skin lighten just a little. She was starting to blush and, judging by the way she pursed her lips, she was having some trouble controlling her reaction to my proximity. The thought encouraged me to take another step closer to sense the heat emanating from her beautiful body. Whatever I was feeling for her was mutual, I just needed to get her to react and reveal it.

"It doesn't take a genius to see what's going on here," I said, assuming a confident tone.

I felt I had the upper hand in this conversation, and I wanted to see what it would lead to. I could sense her pulse racing, blood swishing through her veins like a raging myriad of rivers after a storm. I lowered my head, leaving only a couple of inches of space between our faces. Her lips parted. My heart skipped a beat.

"You clearly have trouble controlling yourself around me, Anjani. Why don't you just give into whatever it is you're feeling?" My tone was low, and our eyes were locked.

"Don't try your charms on me, Jovi, or I'll stop holding my succubus nature in and unleash it on you. Believe me when I say you don't want to play with fire. You will regret ever setting your sights on me," she hissed.

"Why don't you try it?" I dared to say.

"You wouldn't be able to handle it," she muttered and walked past me, toward the mansion entrance.

"You seem to think very little of me, and frankly it's disappointing," I replied, looking over my shoulder.

I didn't mean the last part, but she had this way of riling me up. It was worth it, though. It stopped her in her tracks. She clenched her fists and turned to face me. Her eyes projected death in my direction, and I held my breath for a moment.

I may have just kicked the hornet's nest.

She huffed and came right at me with large, calculated steps. I rooted my right foot into the ground and felt my muscles tense as my body prepared to defend itself against a physical attack.

But she kissed me.

My senses shattered.

Her lips pressed against mine.

I opened my mouth to taste the sweetness. My core incandesced, and my breath stuck in my lungs. I caught her face in my hands and deepened the kiss. She was soft and hungry, and I wanted everything she had to give.

The moment stretched long and hot.

She pushed me away, her lips tender and slightly swollen. Her skin glowed beautifully as she worked hard to catch her breath. I bit into my lower lip and relished in the feeling that washed over me as I looked at her, my eyes fixated on her mouth. Every fiber in my body vibrated, and I felt lightheaded. It dawned on me then that I was euphoric, and it might have had something to do with her succubus nature.

If that's what Anjani in her full form felt like, I wanted more. I was instantly addicted and struggled with a growing tension in both my chest and lower body.

She put on a satisfied smirk, wiping her lips with the back of her hand. Her breathing was uneven, the only sign left to indicate that she was just as aroused as I was, despite her nonchalant attitude designed to make a point.

"See? This is what I meant. Weak." She chuckled and left.

It took me forever to blink again. As I gradually returned to my senses, my feelings emerged with even greater clarity. I was head over heels with this marvelous creature, and I needed her to tell me she felt the same way, because I knew, deep down, that she did.

But I didn't want to be the one chasing her around, like a lovesick puppy, and I wanted her out of her comfort zone, taking the leap along with me. I decided then to let her come to me.

SERENA

Two days had passed since Bijarki had gone through the passage stone to see Hansa. Two very long days that I spent as far away from Draven as possible. He made it easy, though, keeping mostly to himself in his hellish study. I passed the day in the library, reading the many encyclopedias on incubi, Lamias, Dearghs, and many other fascinating creatures of Eritopia, including the extinct storm hounds. The more I learned about the latter, the sorrier I felt that I'd never get the chance to see one.

It was late afternoon when I got out of the library and went looking for Vita. I found her outside in the garden beneath one of the magnolia trees on the front lawn. Tall blades of grass waved in the cool breeze, while the sun set in deep shades of pink and purple.

I sat down next to her. She'd been spending a lot of her time outside, either practicing her fae abilities or tapping into visions of the future. She looked tired, but she wasn't one to give up easily.

"How's it coming along today?" I asked, plucking a small daisy from the ground.

"Not that great, but I'm alternating the sessions," Vita replied with a sigh. "Mornings seem better for fire play. I need more energy to harness the flames and make them obey. I'm making progress on that end, but I think I still have a long way to go before I can do serious damage."

"And the visions? Anything new?"

She shook her head, a frown pulling her slim brows together.

"Not much, just loose little snippets, nothing concrete. Draven said it's natural for the process to be slow, and that I must keep at it. But I admit I'm lacking patience."

The sound of Draven's name made me feel uneasy. My soul was still healing from our last encounter in his study. I had a hard time accepting the situation, and the recurring memories of our moments together weren't helping.

"I'm not fully focused," Vita added. "Bijarki's been gone for two days now, and I don't know if he's okay or when he's coming back. I'm starting to get worried."

Her confession made me push whatever frustration I had with Draven to the back of my head. She was suffering as well. I didn't like seeing her like this. I stood.

"I'll go check with Draven, to see if he knows anything," I said, bracing myself to face him.

Vita looked up, surprise brightening her turquoise eyes.

"Are you sure? You're not on the best terms with the Druid right now. I mean, there's enough tension between the two of you to cut with a knife. It's made breakfast quite awkward over these past couple of days."

"Yes, it's fine. Don't worry about that. I can't do anything about me and him, but I can at least do something about you and the incubus." I sighed and went inside the mansion.

I reached the door to his study and paused, taking a few deep breaths for control. I had to play it as cool as I possibly could. Go in, ask the question, get the answer, leave. It was easy.

I walked in without knocking, as usual. The thought of irritating him even in the smallest of ways gave me some satisfaction. But I stopped as soon as I registered the scene before me.

Draven stood before his desk, a map unraveled beneath his fingers. In front of him stood Hansa and Bijarki. The fire burned hot in the fireplace, making me break into a sweat. Hansa wore her black leather garments with silver plates, and the red cape hung loosely from one shoulder. Her sword's hilt poked out from underneath. She turned around to face me and gave me a beaming, enthusiastic smile, as if I were the best thing she'd seen all day. Bijarki looked over his shoulder and nodded politely.

"Serena!" Hansa exclaimed.

She reached me in two steps and nearly crushed me in a bear

hug, holding me against her toned curves. She was such an impressive creature. I found myself always in awe of her. I hugged her back, taking comfort in her unconditional affection while I caught a glimpse of Draven. Our eyes met for a brief second before he turned his focus back to Bijarki. A muscle danced in his jaw.

"It feels like I haven't seen you in forever," Hansa said and stepped back to look at me.

She scanned me from head to toe and frowned slightly. "You're not eating much, are you?"

"I'm all right. Not much of an appetite, that's all." I blushed and gave her a weak smile. "It's so good to see you. I had no idea you were here or that Bijarki was back."

I made sure to accentuate the incubus's name enough to make him feel singled out. I knew Vita had been worried about him, so it didn't feel right to know he'd been here in Draven's study for who knows how long.

"When *did* you arrive?" I asked Hansa. My gaze found Bijarki, who was giving me a wary sideways glance.

"Oh, about an hour ago. We had to organize everything back at the camp before I could come here," she replied. "I was just briefing the Druid on what we've learned so far."

I nodded and focused on Hansa, unwilling to look at Draven again. I feared that if I saw his deep gray eyes, I would lose control over my senses and cave in. I had to bottle it all in.

"So, what's new?" I asked, a tinge of faux excitement in my voice, as if engaging in the most trivial conversation possible.

"Well, I met Urdi on his mountain. It took me a while to convince him to agree to a meeting with Draven," she said. "He wasn't so happy about Azazel draining his volcanoes of energy for his dark magic, but he was still clinging to that ridiculous pacifist approach of his, according to which everything is the will of Eritopia and Azazel was most likely part of it blah, blah, blah. Long story short, I eventually presented him with the argument that he needed to get really angry and literally catch fire."

She chuckled, remembering the scene. I felt a smile tug at the corners of my mouth. Hansa had that effect on me, apparently.

"They're such peaceful creatures, these Dearghs. Such slow and gentle stone giants…until you make them mad. They light up from the inside like beacons of fire. You must take a few steps back so as not to get scorched. I made him understand that Azazel's use of the volcanoes for his dark magic wasn't natural at all, that it was a Druid-made intervention that contradicted the nature of Eritopia. I had to give him a few examples from the Druids' history for him to better understand what dark magic did. And once he realized that Azazel was killing the Dearghs out of nothing but greed, he lost it," Hansa laughed. "So, Urdi has agreed to meet with Draven at Mount Inon. It's the closest active volcano from here. It's a half-day trip on foot," she concluded.

I nodded slowly, processing all that information and briefly energized by the thought that everything was starting to move along. I could see progress after a few days of stagnation. I'd been bored and restless stuck inside the mansion. I was eager to get out again.

"When are we leaving, then?" I asked.

"You are not going anywhere. You are safer here," Draven interjected before Hansa could reply. "Only myself, Hansa, and Bijarki will be taking this trip. Mount Inon is extremely hazardous."

A moment passed before I let out a mocking laugh. There was no way I would allow him to undermine my presence or my skills ever again. Not after everything we'd been through. He may have intended to protect me by keeping me here, but I represented my friends and my brother in this war. There was no way I'd get left behind.

"Oh no, Draven. I am coming," I replied with the iciest tone I could muster. "Whether you like it or not, I am coming on behalf of my friends, the Oracles you intend to use in this war against Azazel. There will be no further discussion about it."

A moment passed in which no one said anything. Draven just looked at me with his jaw clenched and an unreadable expression on his face. I could see the smirk on Bijarki's face, and I tried hard not to grin back. Hansa stared at me, her white teeth bared in a wide smile. I had impressed her, and that made me feel good.

"We leave in two hours," she said.

"Okay then, if you'll excuse me, I need to go pack a bag." I nodded politely and left.

I closed the study door behind me and exhaled. I'd made it out of there without succumbing to the many emotions rushing through me from being so close to Draven.

Vita

After Serena left, I decided to kill some time in the library. I wasn't getting any visions—I suspected due to my inability to take my mind off Bijarki. So, I figured some reading might help instead. I pulled out a couple of books on Sluaghs and Lamias, along with a history of the incubi nation, and sat at the walnut table in the middle to catch as much of the sunlight pouring into the room as possible.

Half an hour in, I'd learned about the incubi wars from two thousand years ago when the eastern and western citadels had been established as key opposing cities of the two incubi nations, the Bals and the Kerrs. The Bals were known as proud warriors of grand military traditions, while the Kerrs were the textbook definition of democrats, leading through example and progress rather than brute force. It sounded a lot like the human world back home, where freedom and warfare clashed.

The library door opened, and I looked up to see Bijarki come in. My heart jumped, and my limbs softened at the sight of him. He smiled, and relief washed over me as he walked toward me. I straightened my back in response and smiled back.

"You're back," I managed to say.

He nodded and pulled out a chair to sit next to me. The closer he got, the higher my body temperature rose.

"It took me a while. There were a lot of preparations to make with the Red Tribe for what's coming next," he replied.

I realized then that I had missed the sound of his husky voice. My brain responded by sending millions of tingling sensations through my skin.

"Well, you're back in one piece, which is good," I said. "What *is* going to happen next?"

"I'm due to leave again in an hour. We're going to see the Dearghs at Mount Inon. They've agreed to meet with us. I'll be going with Draven, Serena, and Hansa."

"Oh." I nodded.

My enthusiasm quickly fizzled into disappointment. He noticed my frown and cocked his head, giving me a boyish half-smile that spelled mischief.

"I'll be back by tomorrow, little fae," he said. "It's only half a day away."

I had a hard time finding my words, which only added to the frustration brewing inside of me. The more time I spent around Bijarki, the hotter I burned. My body and soul felt helpless before him. I couldn't speak. I was already mentally preparing myself to count more hours before I would see him again.

A few moments passed before he spoke again. "What are you reading?" He glanced at the book before me.

"A history of the incubi," I replied, eyes fixed on the text.

He bent forward enough to scan the text quickly and make my breath hitch. His face was dangerously close to mine again.

"Ah, yes, the Kerrs." He smiled and flipped a couple of pages.

His fingers pointed at another chapter about the allied clans of the Kerrs. I read the first passage, about the Strandh clan, one of the Kerrs' most valuable assets in battle, according to the book. They were known for their physical prowess but also for their ingenious use of technology in combat, including different types of explosive projectiles.

"The Strandh clan." I repeated the name, then looked at Bijarki.

"That's my clan," he said and bit into his lower lip.

Pride glimmered in his silver eyes. I found it enticing and nearly lost myself in his gaze. He told me about the Strandh lineage, renowned for its resilience and strategic thinking.

"My father was once a powerful general of the Kerr nation. He united the southern tribes into one citadel that later pledged its allegiance to the Kerrs," Bijarki added. "That was, of course, before he surrendered to Azazel."

My heart tied itself up in knots at the sight of his pained expression.

"He brought shame to my family, to our entire nation, and to the Strandh lineage."

"I am sorry, Bijarki," I said. "I can only imagine how that must have felt."

My hand instinctively covered his on top of the book, my fingers squeezing gently enough to express some of the affection I felt toward him. He'd shown an emotional side of himself, and, judging by his military upbringing, it had taken an effort for him to open up like that. Even if it was just one expression in front of a little fae.

"I stopped grieving a long time ago, Vita. I'm a soldier. I fight. He's made his bed, and he will have to lie in it."

He took a deep breath and straightened his back, finally noticing my hand on his. I moved to take it back, but he stopped me. His fingers gently brushed my knuckles. His gaze shifted to my face, and our eyes met. I felt my throat dry up, and I licked my lips, unable to stifle the thirst that had suddenly taken over.

He brought his hand up, leaving mine tingling on the book. He cupped my cheek and smiled, his eyelids dropping slowly. He parted his lips as his face came close enough for me to feel his breath over my lips. My heart galloped in my chest. My head swam as I gazed into his eyes, mesmerized by the silver swirls around his pupils.

I felt my lower lip quiver, my core beckoning me to taste him.

Then an image formed in the black pools of his pupils. It grew larger, expanding outward until it enveloped me entirely. Before I knew it, I was standing in the middle of a vision. A dark chamber, made of black stone and heavy iron chains rattling from the ceiling.

Green flames flickered from the wall-mounted torches. I gasped, recognizing the interior of Azazel's castle. My heart stopped at the sight before me. Bijarki was on his knees, his wrists cuffed and bleeding, pulled up by the chains from the ceiling. He was in a lot of pain, bruised and beaten all over, his bare chest slashed diagonally.

A tall incubus walked around him, holding a whip. He was older than Bijarki and bore his physical resemblance. My stomach churned with the realization of who it was.

"You gave up everything for her, son. You stupid, stupid boy," the incubus said to Bijarki.

He struck him. The whistle of the lash cut through the air and bit into Bijarki's back.

I cried out. *Stop it!*

"At least I fought for what I believed in. At least I wasn't a coward who sided with the enemy of my people, of my world, like you did, *father*," Bijarki replied, gritting his teeth from the pain. "At least I fought with honor!"

"Your honor is useless here, son! Your Oracle will rot away in a glass bubble! You have failed, and now I have to convince you to join us, or die!"

Another lash. Another cry.

"Vita!" Bijarki shouted, tears streaming down his cheeks as his father continued to hit him.

His voice echoed through the chamber, and I trembled and cried out.

Stop it!

"Vita?" Bijarki's voice pulled me back into reality.

The image dissipated like a drop of ink in water, swiftly replaced by Bijarki's worried expression. I was lying on the floor in his arms. His hand caressed my face, and his voice gently drew me back into the present.

I breathed a sigh of relief, thankful not to be in that chamber anymore. In that future.

"Are you okay?" he asked, holding me close.

I relaxed in his grip and reached a hand out to touch his face. I saw black runes dancing on my skin again, and I stilled, my fingers on his sharp-edged cheek. He saw them as well and frowned before shifting his focus back to my face.

I watched the runes slowly disappear and took a deep breath. My cheeks burned, and my pulse raced.

"I saw you, Bijarki. You were captured, a prisoner in Azazel's prison. Your own father was punishing you, calling you a failure with each lash of his whip."

I felt his grip tighten. His embrace brought me closer to his face. He nodded and helped me back up on my feet. I wanted to tell him about other visions I'd had of him. I wanted to tell him about the two of us in bed, sleeping blissfully before the Destroyers crashed into the room and tore us apart.

But I wasn't sure whether that had been a vision or a dream. And I lacked the courage to describe such a scene to him. I wasn't used to opening up to people other than my closest family.

"You see the future so that we may prevent it," Bijarki replied.

He ran his fingers through my hair and brushed his knuckles against my cheek. His gaze softened, and his lips stretched into a warm smile.

"Next time I see my father, I'll have to run my sword through him."

He withdrew his hand, bowed curtly, and left the library, while I spent the next few minutes recovering my breath and reeling from the delicious sensations that his touch had ignited in every inch of my flesh.

SERENA

Several hours later, we reached Mount Inon. The journey there had been swift and uneventful. Bijarki and Hansa did a good job of keeping the shape-shifters away with poisoned arrows. The weather was in our favor, and the sun was high in the sky as we climbed the rocky volcano ridge.

It led us to a narrow plateau surrounded by tall shrubs, where giant sculptures adorned the limestone wall of the mountain. Draven and I didn't exchange a single word, and I kept my distance from him, thankful to have Hansa standing between us.

"What now?" I asked her.

She grinned and took a few steps forward.

I took a moment to admire the sculpture. They were twice as

tall as us with sturdy legs, broad shoulders, and red vines crawling up their torsos. It dawned on me then that these were the Dearghs that Aida had described from her vision.

"Wake up, you lazy oafs!" Hansa shouted at the stone giants.

"I don't think they respond to that kind of—" Draven started to say.

The stone began to crackle, and the giants moved.

One by one, they opened their eyes to reveal fiery pupils made of lava and stepped forward with heavy grunts. The biggest one came closer, looking down at us. I couldn't help but tremble. One wrong move and either one of them could crush us with a single blow. My mouth gaped, and my eyes widened as I took in the entire tableau.

"A little respect could get you a long way," the Deargh in the middle said, his voice rumbling like thunder.

"I have no time to caress your ancient egos, Inon," Hansa replied. "We're here to discuss an alliance, as per my conversation with Urdi. Time is running out, so you need to summon the lava boys here tonight!"

A moment passed before Inon spoke again.

"Is this the Druid?" he asked, pointing a lazy finger at Draven.

Hansa nodded.

"Indeed. We've held up our end of the bargain. We're here. It's your turn to come through," she said.

"I thought I smelled a snake," Inon smirked and stepped aside.

The other Dearghs cleared the path for us and, one by one, we entered the mountain through a narrow opening in the wall they had been covering in their statue forms. We reached a tall cave. Its smooth beige walls were riddled with millions of stick figures etched in black and depicting various scenes of hunting, gathering, and prayer. Tiny streams of hot lava ran across the floor, bathing the space in a warm orange light.

I was careful to walk over them as we advanced through the cave.

We stopped in the middle and turned around to face the Dearghs. Inon came forward and spent some time measuring me from head to toe. I was a strange creature to them and not of this world.

"Is this the Oracle?" he asked no one in particular.

"No. My brother is one of the Oracles," I replied.

I didn't know where I'd gathered enough courage to address a Deargh, but Draven's presence so close to me seemed to be a likely source. Somewhere deep inside, I felt like I had to prove to him that I was fearless, unlike him.

"Before I summon my brothers," Inon said. "What is it that you will bring to the table, Druid? Why should we trust you in battle?"

"We have the Oracles and the last Daughter of Eritopia," Draven answered, his chin up. "With the right support from creatures like the Dearghs, the Lamias, and anyone else standing to lose everything if Azazel conquers the whole of Eritopia, we will be able to take him down once and for all."

Inon nodded again.

"But you already know that," Draven added.

Both Hansa and Bijarki turned their heads to look at him, raising their eyebrows.

"I would like to know what else the Dearghs can provide in this battle, other than brute force," he said.

"What do you mean?" Inon replied, tilting his giant stone head to one side.

"Yes, what *do* you mean?" Hansa asked Draven.

"We need to get Sverik, son of Arid, out of Azazel's dungeon. A regular trip there will get us killed, as the Destroyers are getting closer and more aggressive each day, and there are thousands of spies in the jungle, recording every movement that anyone makes through those woods. However, there is an active volcano less than a mile away from that dungeon. We need you to get us there when the time is right," Draven explained.

Inon looked at Draven and smiled.

"You are quite brave to think you could survive such a trip. We are made of lava. It will not burn us. But it will kill you for sure," he replied.

"I'm well aware of that. I'm also aware of the fact that one of the swamp witches' books is with the Dearghs," Draven said, prompting Hansa to stare at him in genuine shock. "The witches were well known for their protective spells against fire. I'm sure there's one in there that we can use."

Silence lingered between them.

"You know about the books?" Hansa asked Draven.

"Of course I do. I have the Oracles, remember?" he replied, then smirked. "I also know you have one too, but we'll talk about that later."

Hansa's skin glowed subtly, reminding me of what she'd told us about the succubi blushing. She'd probably realized that Draven might also have learned about her relationship with his father.

"What will it be, Inon? Will you give us the book?" Draven pressed.

"How did you know we have it?" Inon replied.

"I've done my homework on you, Dearghs. Klibi would have needed some very powerful protection to keep the book hidden and safe from anyone," Draven said. "Mount Inon is the only volcano that creates black diamonds, and there is nothing more powerful, more impervious than that. I had to make a wild guess on this one but given that you've just confirmed it, I'm glad to see I was right."

The Druid wore a smile that spoke of sheer satisfaction. I figured he had his intellectual pride to keep him warm at night, since he'd been so dismissive of me.

Jerk.

"You've assumed well. I'm impressed. Only one who is brave, strong, and patient enough may gain access to the book," Inon explained. "It has been bound by ancient Deargh craft, Druid. Not anyone can get to it, only the worthy, and the black diamond decides who is worthy."

"That's fine. I've been preparing for this battle my entire life.

I'm the one to earn it," Draven replied.

I snorted, amused by his sudden bravery. He stilled and looked over his shoulder, his gray eyes finding mine. Soon enough, all eyes were on me, including the Dearghs'. I sighed, obviously required to explain my reaction in order to not come across as a lunatic.

"Draven will let a gloomy vision of a possible future keep him away from what he wants. I figured that's called being a coward, not someone who is brave, strong, and patient."

The look on Draven's face was priceless. I had really pissed him off, and he couldn't do anything about it. Bijarki smiled mostly to himself, while Hansa pulled herself closer to me, visibly impressed. Any time a woman held her own with a man, even if just with words, she seemed delighted.

"You can try, then," Inon said to me with a half-smile.

I froze. I really didn't think Draven would pull it off. He was scared to get close to me and scared of losing the battle against Azazel. He had said so himself. It was the very opposite of what the Deargh had described as prerequisites to get the book, and we couldn't afford any kind of failure at this point.

"That's not going to happen," Draven interjected before I could open my mouth. "She's in no way qualified to do this."

And that was enough to make me snap and think with my pride, rather than my brain. I stepped forward, bumping into his shoulder as I stopped in front of Inon. My newfound courage, fueled by childish pride, was enough to make me take the lead.

"My friends, my family, my whole world depends on me right

now. I'll do it," I said.

"Serena, this is dangerous. Don't be foolish," Draven replied.

"Oh, please. Between the two of us, I'm the one with the spine," I shot back with a sideways glance.

"Serena, maybe you shouldn't," Hansa interjected.

"I have to! I have everything to lose in this war unless I get that book! We need all the help we can get!"

She sighed, and the shadow of a smile passed over her face. She understood what was at stake. With each second that passed, the more convinced I was that I had to do this. Not just to prove to Draven that I had more courage than he did, but to prove to my friends and my brother that they could rely on me in the darkest of times.

"So it shall be, then," Inon proclaimed.

He guided us through a tunnel that took us deeper into the mountain. It ended in a massive black marble wall. I was first in line behind him when he placed his hand on the wall and muttered something under his breath. The wall trembled and slid to the right, granting us access to a small chamber.

Inon walked inside, clearing the path for me to see inside. The walls were smooth and black, reflecting everything inside. Thin cracks scattered across the floor, allowing the lava beneath to shine its amber light into the chamber.

In the middle, resting on a black marble cube, was a black diamond box, its edges polished to perfection. Inon stood next to it.

"The box will ask you questions. If you answer truthfully, it will give you the book. If you lie or give half-truths, it will seal you in this chamber until you die without food or water," he said solemnly.

I needed a minute to fully process the terms of this trial. Was I really ready to risk my life like that?

Draven came up behind me, placing his hand on my shoulder.

"Serena, please don't do this," he told me.

I could sense the urgency in his voice, the trembling pitch. His fear for my safety only fueled my determination. I pushed him away. I stepped forward and entered the room. Inon left and stood beyond the entrance with Draven next to him.

I looked over my shoulder and saw the Druid's face mortified by despair. He shook his head. "Serena, please."

"Somebody needs to teach you how to stand up for those you love, so it might as well be me, Druid."

I was shocked by my own brazenness toward him. Where did all that come from?

The black marble wall slid back into place, sealing me away from the rest of the world. I would have enough time to answer that question later. I took a deep breath and looked at the black diamond box.

"Okay then, let's do this," I said, mostly to myself, wondering if the box would respond.

Aida

I spent most of my time in the attic, constantly working through snippets of visions. Most of them were useless, as I was unable to hold on for long enough to see more.

I delved deep into a state of relaxation, sitting in a meditation pose and carefully measuring my breaths. Another vision began to unfurl before my eyes. Inside Azazel's dungeons, Marchosi stumbled along a black stone hallway lit by green fires overhead. He had trouble standing up, constantly shifting from Druid to serpent form, unable to keep himself steady.

Beads of sweat dripped from his forehead. He scratched his neck where dark green scales spread out like a rash. He cursed and punched at the walls until he reached a wide chamber swarming with Destroyers. They all looked at him and hissed, grinning from ear to ear.

"You're having trouble staying in Druid form, huh?" one of them asked, his voice oozing contempt.

"That's what you get when you stand too close to Azazel," another one cackled.

"He corrupts, he soils, he breaks our very nature until we turn into this," a third one added, gesturing at his own body, the lower half a full serpent tail, thick and scaly.

Marchosi heaved as he stood up, leaning against the wall, fury marring his once handsome features. He pulled a piece of parchment from his belt and threw it on the floor. It unraveled, revealing a map with a specific area circled in blood.

"Lead a purge on that location," he barked at them. "Azazel wants whatever is in it dead."

I stepped toward the map, but before I could see it in full detail, the vision dissolved, and I woke up lying on the floor, breathing heavily. A tortuous sigh left my chest. I rolled over to the side, where a sheet of paper and a piece of charcoal waited. I made a few notes of the runes fluttering across my arms before they faded away.

They were never a pretty sight, but I'd gotten relatively used to them, enough to no longer break into a sweat when I saw them.

I sat up and nearly jumped out of my skin at the sight of Field sitting on a crate, a few feet away from me, watching. He'd been so quiet. Concern drew a frown on his face.

"How long have you been sitting there?" I asked.

"I should ask you the same question. You look so pale."

"I'm okay, Field. Just a little annoyed because I can't hold on to these visions for as long as I'd like," I replied.

A moment passed. His gaze didn't leave my face. His expression was firm and unreadable.

"You need some fresh air," he said.

I nodded my agreement. It was getting pretty stuffy in there, despite the open windows. Just having him close to me was sending my body heat soaring again.

"I definitely do," I mumbled mostly to myself.

He stood up and reached me in a few wide steps. Before I could say or do anything, Field picked me up in his arms and carried me out to the ledge of the roof through the middle window. I held on for dear life, my arms coiled around his neck, and my body soft against his.

I yelped when I looked down and saw the garden beneath. If we fell...

"What are you doing?" I asked.

He gave me one of his signature smirks and jumped. I gasped and tightened my grip, hiding my face in his chest as I heard his wings fan out and flap a couple of times. I opened my eyes as the air brushed against my face.

We flew high above the jungle surrounding the mansion, beneath a gorgeous pink and orange sunset. We circled the area for a while before Field gently placed me on top of a purple tree. I straddled the thick branch with my legs and took a deep breath, enjoying the view and the humming in the lower half of my body. He had that effect on me.

He settled in front of me, placing the weight of his torso onto his arms.

"Thank you," I said. "Didn't know I needed that."

His lips stretched into a satisfied grin, his eyes flickering with something akin to fire. His black hair fell in lazy strands, framing his beautiful face and contrasting with his sharp cheekbones.

"What have you been seeing?" he asked, watching me carefully.

I told him about my most recent vision of Marchosi, and he looked out to the west. The setting sun reflected its amber glow in his irises.

"Who knows where the Destroyers are going? With how hell-bent Azazel is on conquering this entire world, I'm pretty sure anyone is fair game," Field said, his voice low.

He then turned his attention back on me. "Why didn't you tell me how you felt?"

I blanked completely. My eyes went wide, and my mouth dropped open. I didn't see that question coming, and I had no idea how to respond. Did he know? How did he know? Did someone tell him? The girls, maybe?

A million thoughts ran through my head.

He tilted his head and looked at me with an expression that made every thought in my brain scatter.

"I—I don't know what you're talking about. What…what do you mean? I don't—I don't feel anything…I…uh…"

I was stunned by his proximity and the two pools of blue-green splendor that seemed to see right into my soul. He drew his face closer to mine, a smile slowly revealing his perfect teeth.

I was unable to think anymore as his lips almost touched mine.

My whole body shook with emotion. My breath stuck in my throat, and my heart exploded in my chest. I was so nervous and out of control that I shifted my weight a little, hopefully enough to make myself look less rattled.

But I jerked my hip a little too much. I lost my balance and fell off the branch.

I shrieked.

Field caught me before I hit the branches beneath and held me tight as he flew us back to the mansion.

I trembled in his arms, infuriated by my own knee-jerk reaction, convinced that I had ruined what could have been our first kiss. I cursed under my breath as Field landed us on the grass outside the plantation house.

I avoided looking at him out of pure embarrassment and moved to stand on my own. But my legs were jelly and undermined my dignity. I nearly fell again. Field wrapped me in an embrace, his firm grip holding me against his hard body.

My eyes met his, and I melted. A strange pressure built up in my throat.

His gaze softened, and the turquoise in his eyes turned a shade darker. The corner of his mouth turned upward.

"You know, you're a funny, clumsy little thing," he quipped, his voice low and raspy. "Here I am trying to kiss you, and you keep falling out of my reach."

His words knocked the breath out of me more than my fall. I stilled, my lips parting slowly.

And then he bent down, and the next thing I knew he was kissing me. Time stopped. His mouth took over mine, demanding that I give him everything. His lips were soft and moist. His tongue found mine as he explored everything I had to give.

I moaned gently, and he tightened his grip, keeping me close enough to feel his heartbeat echoing into my chest. Heat spread through my body, and I gave in completely as he deepened the kiss.

I felt a tear leave my eye as I surrendered my senses to sheer bliss.

A darkness enveloped us as his wings stretched out and covered us, giving us privacy from the rest of the world. It was just me and him, lost in each other, our lips and our souls fusing.

I had waited a lifetime for this.

Phoenix

I woke up in the middle of the night from what felt like a horrible nightmare. My subconscious was signaling my underlying fear of losing the last Daughter of Eritopia. I had dreamed of her sisters coming to us, with their violet eyes and their golden masks, and taking her away. I couldn't stand the idea. It felt as if a knife had been driven into my chest again. The pain was unbearable and seared through my consciousness.

I sat up, breathing heavily. I wiped the sweat off my face and looked around my room, which was covered in darkness except one corner by the window, where the pearly light of the moon shone down on an armchair where the Daughter had fallen asleep. Her arms were wrapped around her legs, keeping her knees close to her chest. A waterfall of reddish pink hair poured over her shoulders and back.

My chest burned at the sight of her.

I got up and scooped her into my arms, unwilling to let her sleep in that uncomfortable position. Clearly, she didn't want to sleep in her own room.

I laid her on the bed and pulled the duvet over to keep her warm. I got in and settled on my side, my back to her. I quietly counted my breaths. With her body so close to mine, my senses were playing tricks on me. My heart thudded.

I heard her moan and shift behind me. Soon enough, I felt her breath on the back of my neck and a delicious heat spread through my limbs. I focused on my pulse, alarmed by how my blood raced through my veins.

I gave in and turned to face her. She slept so peacefully with her head resting on the pillow. I took the whole picture of the Daughter in, feature by feature—her beautiful face, her soft lips the color of red wine, her small nose and delicate eyebrows. They all spoke of perfection.

I longed to feel her lips on mine. What would she taste like?
Probably heaven.

I fell asleep watching her, asking myself how I'd gotten to this point, from messing around in Hawaii to having my lifeline so irrevocably tied to this one, extraordinary creature.

SERENA

I had no measure of time inside that chamber. All around me was luscious black marble. Deep cracks in the floor revealed the burning hot lava below. The air was surprisingly cool, despite the heat seeping from beneath.

I walked around for a while, occasionally glancing at the box, wondering what I had to do to get it to open. Inon hadn't been specific.

My mind constantly darted toward where Draven was probably standing on the other side of the wall, frustrated out of his mind. Despite the uncertainty of my own situation I felt an ounce of satisfaction at the thought of him thinking about me in my absence. It was selfish, but it soothed my bruised ego.

Soon enough, my patience wore thin.

"Hello?" I asked, hoping the black diamond box might answer. "I'm here for the book. Can I have it?"

Nothing.

"The fate of Eritopia hangs in the balance, and I can help, but I need the swamp witches' book."

Yet more silence ensued.

I frowned and approached the box. It sat on a black marble cube at eye level. I looked at it from various angles, but nothing seemed out of the ordinary or out of place.

I reached out and touched one side, its cold surface sending a shiver down my spine.

It clicked.

I jumped back and watched a map of bright orange lines crossing it like tiny rivers of lava flowing carelessly all over the smooth black diamond. Its facets lit up, revealing its content beneath layer upon layer of hard, crystallized carbon. There was a book inside, bound in leather.

The box was showing me what was inside, and I held my breath with excitement.

It seemed to respond to my touch, so I pressed my finger against one side again.

The little orange veins pulsated with light in response.

"Who are you?" A soft voice echoed in my head, resonating deep in my bones.

"I am Serena Hellswan," I answered.

"What do you want?"

"I want the book."

So far, the questions seemed basic. Perhaps I wouldn't rot in here after all.

"Why do you want the book?"

"Because I need it to save Eritopia."

"Why do you need to save Eritopia?"

"Because it's in danger. You might not know it, but there's a crazed Druid out there killing everyone in his path and burning everything down."

"Why do *you* need to save Eritopia?"

"It's not just me," I replied. "There are more with me, Oracles, incubi, succubi, a Druid, my friends, the Dearghs outside this room. We all need to save Eritopia."

"Why are you here?"

I thought that one over for a second, convinced I'd already answered.

"I'm here for the book, I told you."

"Why do you want the book?"

It sounded a little too repetitive for my frayed nerves. I took a deep breath.

"Because I need to save Eritopia."

"Why you?"

I sighed, beginning to understand why Inon had mentioned patience as a prerequisite to obtaining the book.

"Because it had to be me."

A moment passed before the voice sounded again in my head, like a distant memory.

"What will you give in return for the book?"

"Whatever I can."

"That is not enough."

"Then what do you want from me?"

"What are you willing to give?"

I ran my fingers through my hair. It seemed I was in for a long ride.

SERENA

I spent a long time doing this back and forth with the box. I was thirsty, hungry, and pacing the room nervously, answering the same string of questions over and over, leading me to the same ending.

I was exhausted. It had been so long that I dozed off on the floor between questions, but I couldn't tell for how many hours. I woke up, realizing that I was still stuck in the chamber with the black diamond box staring down at me, patiently waiting for my answers. And I tried again and again and again. My eyes stung, my head hurt, and the more time passed, the more drained I felt.

I struggled with different emotional stages, from anger and frustration to hopelessness and despair. I raked my brain for reasonable arguments to convince the box to open, but it didn't respond. It threw me for yet another loop.

In the absence of a clock, it felt like time had deliberately slowed down, just to make things worse.

"What are you willing to give in return for the book?"

I had promised fealty, favors, my own blood, anything that could get me closer to getting that book out of that wretched black diamond box. But it wouldn't budge. All roads ended here.

"What are you willing to give in return for the book?"

"Again, I ask, what do *you* want me to give in return for the book? Name your price!"

"This is not about what I want. It's about what you want to give. How much is Eritopia worth to you?"

"It's a world full of creatures who deserve to live. What value can I place on an entire world?!"

"Do you want Eritopia to live?"

"Yes," I sighed.

"Give me a reason."

"Because everyone deserves a chance at life, and it shouldn't be determined by a monster like Azazel. He has no right to do what he's doing."

"Why do you want Eritopia to live? It's not your world, is it?"

I scoffed. Deep inside, I understood the point that the box, as annoyingly sentient as it seemed, was trying to make.

"I don't have to belong to this world to want to save it. Life is precious everywhere and in all of its forms."

A long silence followed, as if it waited for a more complete answer.

"If I don't save Eritopia, my own planet will perish. The death of Eritopia means the death of everyone and everything I hold dear," I said.

A beat.

"So, then, what are you willing to sacrifice in order to save Eritopia?" The words were the same, but the tone was deeper now, as if it was only now getting serious.

I started considering the grim options, which I had avoided entirely throughout the time I'd been in that chamber. But it seemed as though I was running out of time, and desperate measures were due. I thought about what I could live without, and my stomach churned painfully.

"You can have my eyesight," I said.

"Your eyesight to save a world? Do you feel that's enough?"

"My arms. My legs. My voice. You pick! Just take something!"

"This is not a meat market. You don't just offer up a piece of yourself thinking it will get you what you want. It does not work like that. What are you willing to give in return for the book? What is the absolute value that you place on its use toward saving Eritopia?"

"It's essential to saving Eritopia!"

"Is it worth just your eyesight. Or a finger? Or your leg?"

It dawned on me then that I wasn't being entirely honest with myself. I knew, deep down, that the book was worth more than I was willing to give, even if that included my limbs or any of my senses. It was probably worth more than I was.

More time passed in utter silence, as I gradually succumbed to a new feeling. I despised that box. It made me queasy.

"What do you think is the right price for the book?" I tried again.

"I cannot tell you that. *You* must tell *me*. What will you give in return for the book?"

I caved in, overwhelmed by desperation. I fell to my knees, letting out all the anger and fear that had been mounting inside of me since the first day I had set foot in Eritopia. I had pushed it all back, focusing on anything else that would get me through to the next day.

But I couldn't do it any longer. Not like that. My anguished cry echoed through the chamber.

I had to face the hard and painful truth. A sacrifice would have to be made for this.

I had to be ready to give anything and everything in order to bring down Azazel and save my brother, my friends, and the billions both in this world and mine.

"I will give anything... I will sacrifice everything, even myself, if you release the book so my friends can use it to rid Eritopia of the disease that is Azazel."

Hot tears streamed down my cheeks. I had been in here for so long, I would either die of starvation or die getting that book out of its box. Whichever way this went, I braced myself for my own end. Resignation was not something I'd ever been used to, but when it came, I felt enlightened. I barely recognized myself.

"I'm ready to give my life for a greater purpose." I sighed, leaning forward and shuddering from crying hiccups.

"You are willing to sacrifice yourself to save Eritopia?"

"Yes… Yes, I am… I truly am…"

An excruciatingly long second passed before the box finally replied.

"What about the Druid?"

"What… What?"

I blinked several times and stood, my mind blank and eyes stinging.

"How will he live without you?" the box asked.

What did it know? How much did it know? What was the purpose of such a question?

"What do you know about the Druid?" I replied, squinting my eyes.

"How will he live without you?"

"You didn't answer my question!"

"I'm not here to answer your question. You are here to answer mine."

I wasn't going to win this one.

I took a deep breath and went for complete honesty, suspecting that the box could read my mind. It was already tuned to my honesty, given the long winding road that had led me up to this moment.

"Neither I nor Draven matter much in the face of the darkness that is about to swallow Eritopia. The Druid will have to live on without me if need be."

"Are you sure he will be able to live on without you?"

"What kind of question is that?! He will have to!"

I choked on another wave of tears and swallowed as much of it back as I could. My heart was torn and twisted, my stomach in a lot of pain, my lips dry and crusty.

There comes a point when one accepts the inevitable fate drawn out before them, my father had once said to me. I saw him clearly in my mind, alongside my mother, my grandparents, and our entire family back in The Shade.

At least they didn't know I existed. At least they wouldn't suffer.

"Just end it already and kill me. Give us the book."

Silence.

I let out another sigh, feeling my shoulders slump. The prospect of dying wasn't something I was comfortable with, not in the least. But if I was to go, I'd go on my terms.

"Just kill me! I'm ready! Kill me!"

"Your willingness to sacrifice yourself for something greater than your own desires is what will bring you victory. Only in the face of death does one see that. There comes a point when one accepts the inevitable fate drawn out before them—"

"—and that is where true strength lies. In sacrifice." I completed the box's sentence.

I was stunned. How was it quoting my father?

The box clicked again, and the front side fell forward on the black marble surface. It granted me access to the book.

I stood there, breathing heavily as I reviewed everything that I had said and heard in that chamber, retracing every step that had led me to this point. I had no idea what I had gotten myself into walking in, but, as relief of cosmic proportions washed over me, I realized that I knew exactly what I was walking out to.

I reached out and took the book with trembling fingers, caressing its leather cover and smelling the musky pages inside. I cried again, this time tears of joy and relief, understanding that it had all been a test to prove my strength.

A cruel, but effective test. My mind was clear, and my heart was stronger than I had thought.

I heard the wall slide behind me with a long crackling sound.

I turned around and saw Inon standing at the back of the tunnel. Hansa and Bijarki sat on the floor. Draven was slumped on the side in front of a small oil lamp. Its flame flickered timidly in the semi-darkness. They looked exhausted, and I wondered how long they'd been there.

At the sound of the wall clicking open, they all looked up. Draven was the first to dart up and run at me. His beautiful eyes filled with tears as he took me in his arms and squeezed me. His breath was ragged, and his voice was raw. I dropped the book.

"I thought you were dead," he gasped, tightening his grip while his hands ran up and down my back, as if desperate to feel every inch of me.

I melted in his arms, overcome by a million emotions at once. I saw Hansa and Bijarki beaming at me, a tear rolling down the succubus's cheek. She quickly wiped it away with the back of her hand. A chief could not be seen crying, I figured.

"You've been in there for two days, Serena," Draven's voice poured into my ears, soothing my soul. "I've tried everything I possibly could to get you out of there. All the magic in the world couldn't work… I…I tried…I even tried brute force. Nothing worked…"

There was so much pain in his voice that it hurt me to hear it. He had suffered enough, helpless on the other side of the wall. I responded to his embrace and sighed with all the air that my lungs could gather and moaned softly against his broad chest.

I had missed him. I had missed his strength, his hardness, his soft voice.

He pulled back to look at me, his eyes blinking black, his gray irises glimmering with a mixture of pain and happiness and something else I couldn't quite put my finger on. His gaze softened, and his lips crashed down on mine. He kissed my mouth hard, then my cheeks, my forehead, the tip of my nose. He dropped a hundred kisses all over my face, settling over my lips again for a deeper experience.

I opened myself up to him and took it all in.

"I'm so sorry, Serena," he whispered between kisses. "I was foolish to think I could live without feeling you in my arms, against my skin, on my lips… Please, forgive me."

I burst into tears. I was so weak; my knees gave out as he held me up. Thirst, hunger, and a million other feelings all crashed down on me at once. I gripped his shirt and cried into his chest, letting it all out—all the pain, the anguish I had felt in his absence, the grief I'd experienced in front of imminent death, all of it. I breathed it all out, sob after sob.

"Don't leave me again, Draven," I whimpered. "Don't push me away like that again."

He groaned and scooped me up in his arms. I felt so light and limp.

I rested my head against his shoulder and closed my eyes.

I was finally free.

SERENA

I passed out as soon as Draven picked me up in his arms. They shook me back to consciousness, enough for me to eat a few pieces of bread and drink some water. I fell asleep after that.

I peeled my eyes open a few hours later. I was lying in a makeshift bed of animal furs with soft leaves underneath, a fire burning close to me. Bijarki had set up camp inside one of the caves that the Dearghs had offered us for shelter.

I saw him sitting by the fire next to Anjani and Draven.

I tried to move, but I was too drowsy, so I decided to keep still and listen. My body was weakened to the point where not even food or water could help. I'd have to syphon off someone soon to regain my strength.

Draven was looking through the book, amber flames throwing a playful light against the shadows beneath his cheeks. I felt warmth flowing through my body at the sight of him, my heart blossoming and expanding like a star, burning everything in its path.

"From what I can tell," he mused while flipping the pages, "the spells are incomplete. I get the feeling that the three books that the swamp witches made work together or don't work at all."

"So, they're useless if taken separately," Hansa concluded, chewing on a piece of dried meat.

"Indeed. The witches were the brightest of Eritopia for a long time before Azazel found a way to wipe them out," Draven replied.

"In that case, we need to go back to my tribe and get the second book."

"We need to get there fast, though," Bijarki interjected. "It's a long walk from here."

"The Dearghs can give us some of their horses. They run wild all around the mountain," Hansa replied.

Draven glanced over to me and saw me awake. His expression softened, and he set the book aside and came over to check on me.

"Are you okay?" he asked, his voice low.

I gave him a weak smile, and he lay down in front of me, wrapping his arms around my waist. I wondered what Hansa and Bijarki were thinking at the sight of us. Draven held me tight, and I relaxed against his body, feeling his heartbeat against the palms of my hands.

"I'm not letting go of you again, just so we are clear," he

whispered and dropped a hot kiss on my forehead.

"I feel weak," I mumbled.

He looked down at me, concern drawing a frown on his beautiful face.

"You can feed off me, Serena. I need you at full strength."

Our eyes met, and I felt my soul open up before him. I cupped his face in my hands, giving in to the sentry hunger, and drew all the energy that he offered. Ribbons of gold flowed into me, replenishing my body better than any slice of bread. I felt all of Draven pouring into me. Warmth and affection filled my chest. I closed my eyes.

I tasted bliss as I drifted off to sleep.

SERENA

I woke up fully refreshed and feeling ready to take on the whole world. Draven's seemingly endless supply of heady and sunny energy had brought me back to life and had even given me an extra kick, like a cup of deliciously hot coffee.

We galloped through the jungle, riding the gorgeous mustangs that the Dearghs had summoned for us. They were graceful creatures with incredible strength and stamina, and they seemed to fly across the many miles between Mount Inon and the Red Tribe.

It took us a few hours, but as the sun settled at the highest point in the sky, we saw the limestone wall about a hundred yards away, that little bit of swamp witch magic that kept the succubi camp hidden from the rest of the world.

My horse raced graciously alongside Draven's, and we occasionally glanced at each other, exchanging a thousand unspoken words along the way. Whatever I was feeling for him, it would only get stronger. His energy was addictive. His touch sent me spiraling toward ecstasy each time. I craved the feeling of his lips on mine, and I relished each gaze he directed at me. I swooned over the man he was, his strength, his insecurity, his knowledge, and his power. I adored how we delighted and annoyed each other, how the smallest of moments could draw us even closer to one another.

Whatever this was brewing between us, it was just beginning, and I smiled. I knew for sure that I wanted more. I wanted everything.

As our horses reached the limestone wall, I was hit by a sudden feeling of uneasiness.

Something felt wrong. Horribly wrong.

The wall was torn down, chunks of stone scattered all around.

The succubi camp fanned out beyond, still and quiet, thick black columns of smoke rising from multiple fires.

"NO!" Hansa shouted and jumped off her horse.

I felt queasy as I got off and walked toward the scene in front of us. Draven and Bijarki followed.

Hansa jumped over the broken limestone and ran into her camp. A tragedy unraveled in front of us. Dozens of succubi lay dead on the ground, arrows and swords sticking out of their bodies. Silver blood glazed the dark red grass. Tents had burned down.

The smell was unbearable, a mixture of charred flesh and burnt hair.

My stomach turned, and I felt a wave of nausea taking over. I struggled to walk forward.

Draven came next to me, his arm stretching to keep me close. I leaned into him and looked at every single element that was part of the horrific composition. Bijarki ran ahead, looking for survivors.

The camp had been attacked. I recognized the arrows stuck in some of the succubi. Destroyer arrows. They had found the Red Tribe somehow, and they'd had no interest in leaving any prisoners.

Hansa found one of her generals barely alive, her stomach riddled with Destroyer arrows. She fell on her knees and pulled her sister's head onto her lap, her face pained and lower lip trembling uncontrollably.

"Who did this?!" Hansa asked the dying succubus, who kept coughing silver blood.

"Sluaghs…found us… They came with Destroyers… Sluaghs on the ground with swords and axes, Destroyers above with their arrows and spears… Early morning when we were sleeping… Didn't stand a chance…"

I froze and felt Draven stiffen next to me.

Bijarki came back, slowly shaking his head. "None left alive."

The general heaved and gave her last breath, dying in Hansa's arms.

I then realized how difficult the road ahead would be. Azazel had found the Red Tribe and had killed them all without hesitation or any interest in taking any of them prisoner. My heart sank at the sight of Hansa in so much pain.

I had seen her suffer before when she lost three scouts to the Destroyers at Arid's camp, but this was a whole new level of devastation. In just one raid, the Destroyers had managed to wipe out the entire Red Tribe. I couldn't begin to imagine how she must feel.

Hansa's breathing hastened. She seemed close to hyperventilating. She let out the most heartbreaking and excruciating roar I had ever heard in my life.

Birds scattered out of the dark forests covering the northern mountain ridges.

I felt Draven's fingers dig into my arm.

The Red Tribe was gone, and our alliance with the other creatures of Eritopia seemed more fragile than ever.

And by the looks of it, Azazel was only just getting started.

READY FOR MORE?

Dear Shaddict,

Thank you for reading *A Meet of Tribes*.

The next book, **_ASOV 46_** is called **_A Ride of Peril_**, and it releases **June 27th, 2017**!

Visit: www.bellaforrest.net for details.

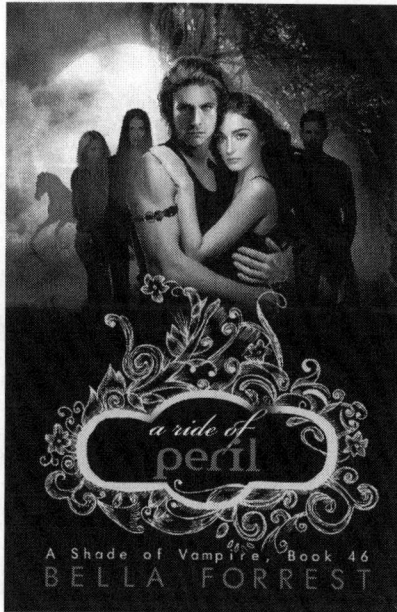

I'm extremely excited to see you there!

Love,

Bella xxx

P.S. Join my VIP email list and I'll send you a personal reminder as soon as I have a new book out. Visit here to sign up: **www.forrestbooks.com**

(Your email will be kept 100% private and you can unsubscribe at any time.)

P.P.S. At the end of this ebook, I've included a Novak family tree.

P.P.P.S. Follow The Shade on Instagram and check out some of the beautiful graphics: @ashadeofvampire

You can also come say hi on Facebook: www.facebook.com/AShadeOfVampire

And Twitter: @ashadeofvampire

NOVAK FAMILY TREE

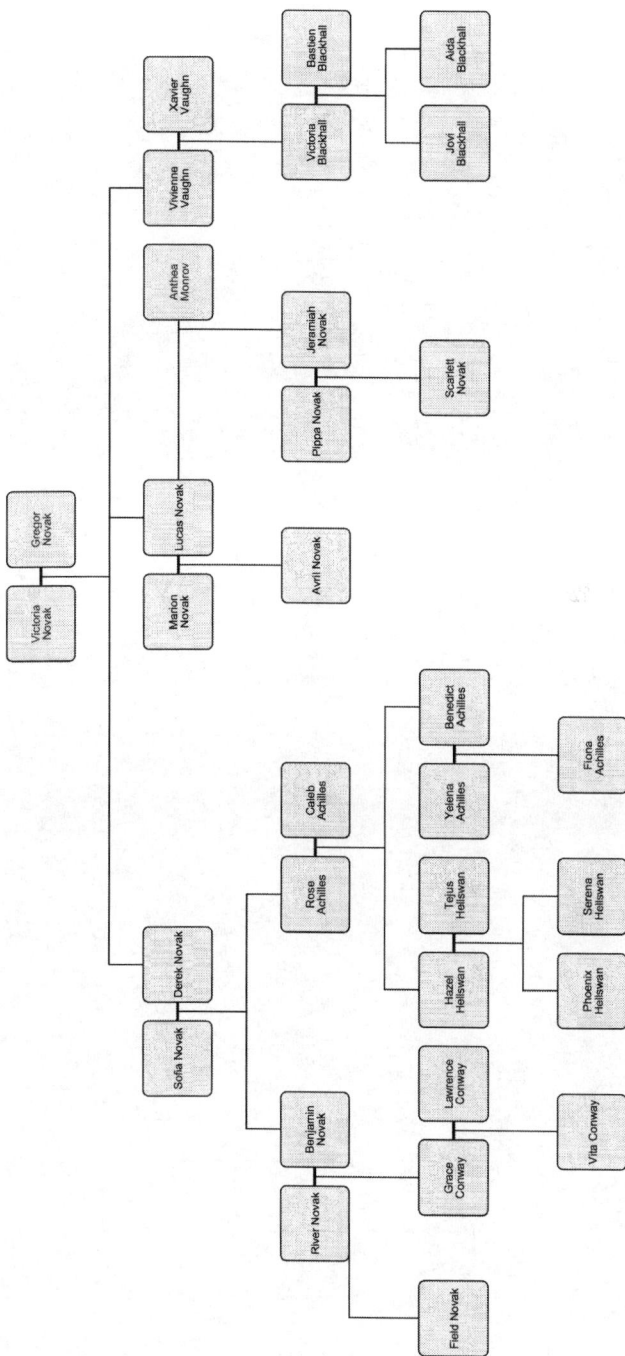

Made in the USA
Columbia, SC
14 June 2017